LOVE IS SWEET

COULD IT BE LOVE?

NICKI GRACE

ISBN: 9798528426297

Copyright © 2021 by Nicki Grace Novels

All rights reserved.
No part of this book may be reproduced in any form or by any electronic or
mechanical means, including information storage and retrieval systems,
without written permission from the author, except for the use of brief
quotations in a book review.

To anyone who has experienced the roller coaster of love I hope you found your happiness and if not, I'm sure it's on the way.

CHAPTER 1

P iper was stuck and panicking for a way out. It was just her luck that something so ridiculous would happen. How in the hell did one get their clothes jammed into an escalator, anyway? Opting to wear a long, flowy beach skirt instead of shorts was how it happened.

But right now, that didn't matter; escaping this mess was the top priority. If a solution didn't reveal itself by the time she got to the bottom. Her skirt was going to be yanked off of her body, taking her pride with it.

Crossing her purse strap over her chest, Piper tugged at the skirt for the fifth time, attempting to work it loose. Still, it didn't budge. Looking around nervously, she spotted a guy stepping onto the escalator. Mentally calculating his distance, he must have been approximately seven steps behind her.

The escalator was long—maybe close to 50 or so of those metallic death traps called stairs. The long-range from top to bottom should be good news, but the reality was, there could be 1,000 stairs, and still, the end would come too soon.

Thinking fast, she waved at the guy. He looked at her and pointed to himself.

Nodding frantically, Piper motioned for him to come down. Hurrying towards her, he immediately saw the predicament.

"Can you help me pull it loose?"

The guy yanked at the base of the floral garment while Piper pulled from higher up; however, it remained locked in place.

"Shit! It's stuck in there good."

"I know," Piper said, glancing around at just how big of a crowd she was about to flash. There weren't many people, and thankfully, she had worn cute underwear. At least some of the advice her aunt gave her had stuck.

Then with horror, she realized that wasn't true. She was on her period, which meant underneath this skirt wasn't sexy lace but underwear that resembled a granny's taste.

They were big, white, saggy, and sported a hole on the side that made her appear like she was unkempt and unloved, when in truth, they were the most comfortable pair of underwear she owned.

"Okay, I have an idea," he said.

Piper felt her hopes rise. She would be on board with just about anything at this point.

The guy removed his book bag and then his jacket. Tossing his book bag back onto one shoulder, he held out his jacket to her.

"Put my jacket around your waist and zip it up. Then, remove your skirt before it gets ripped off."

The plan sounded pretty solid. The bottom wasn't far away, and there was no time to waste coming up with an alternative. Moving faster than she thought possible, Piper pulled the jacket around her waist, zipped it, then tied the sleeves, securing a knot in front of her.

Unfastening the skirt, it slunk down around her ankles, and she began stepping out of it. Piper barely managed to remove one foot before the stairs flattened and tugged the skirt with a powerful force, causing her to trip.

At the last second, the guy lifted her, pulling her entangled foot free and her mind out of panic mode. He steadied her, and still holding onto his arms, Piper spared a glance back at the escalator. The skirt had been ripped clean through, with a small piece being set free as the rest of the thin floral fabric was taken underneath the mechanical stairs. This was all so embarrassing.

Picking up a small piece that managed to escape, Piper sighed. That was one of her favorite skirts. Shoving what was left into her purse, Piper turned to face the kind stranger.

He was surprisingly cute. Tall, slim with boyish good looks.

"Thank you. I'm Piper Fosters," she said, offering her hand.

"Scott Bolden."

He gave her a smile that made her weak at the knees. He possessed intense dark eyes that somehow made her feel wanted and admired.

Piper broke eye contact first. Spending all day staring at this attractive man would have been fun, but she had to get to Jake, the four-year-old that she babysat once a week.

"There's a souvenir shop over there—"

"You can keep the jacket—"

They both blurted out at the same time.

Scott apologized.

"I'm sorry, beautiful; what were you saying?"

Beautiful, huh? She thought.

She liked where this was going. Scott was attracted to her, and the feeling was most definitely mutual.

Piper licked her lips flirtatiously.

"I was saying that there is a souvenir shop over there. I might be able to find some leggings and give you back your jacket."

"Alright, lead the way."

Taking her first step, Piper stopped as realization set in. Adjustments to her usual stride would be necessary since walking in a zipped-up jacket was more restrictive than a dress or jeans. Taking smaller steps to account for the limitation, Piper swiftly found her rhythm and prayed she didn't look like a penguin scurrying along.

"So, Piper, what brings you to the Atlanta Airport?"

"I live here. I'm returning from a mini beach vacation in Miami. Hence, the floral skirt that the escalator just ate."

It was mostly the truth and the only part of her trip she was willing to share.

"Yikes, what a way to return from vacation, huh? Minding your own business, and then the escalator takes your clothes."

Piper shrugged.

"I wear less at my night job."

"And what exactly is your night job?"

"I'm a retired stripper."

Scott's eyebrows shot up as he stopped to look at Piper.

"Really?"

"I know what you're thinking. The word retired makes me sound so old, but I swear I'm only 26."

He laughed, picking up on her sense of humor.

"I'm 30, and that's not exactly what I was thinking. But seriously, you used to strip for a living?"

"Technically, I still do it. I'm finishing up several more shows before I officially cease flaunting my birthday suit for cash. But during the day, I'm an administrative assistant for a veterinary clinic."

"Very interesting. I'll bet you look good on stage."

"Wouldn't you like to know?" she said with a wink.

The look in his eyes gave her the confirmation she expected. Of course, he would like to see her on stage; he had a pulse. His desire didn't bother her as long as he brought his wallet. Stripping was a job where the employees favorited cash bonuses just like any other.

People were often surprised by how open she was about being a stripper. Sure, in a job interview leading with that information was frowned upon, but in unprofessional settings, hiding what she did for a living wasn't her style.

Stripping wasn't some dirty little secret that produced feelings of shame. Piper enjoyed her time on the stage, and contrary to what people thought, she wasn't an easy lay or an airhead.

For the most part, she had raised herself and learned a lot about life, love, and relationships in the process. Even though she had made some poor choices in men, Piper's list of sex partners could be counted on one hand.

"Anyway, Scott. Thanks for saving me. I don't expect people at the airport would have tipped very well for the show."

"I love how down-to-earth you seem. Most women I meet don't have a sense of humor."

"Maybe you've been meeting the wrong women?"

"Maybe I have," Scott agreed.

Piper knew for a fact that she'd been dating the wrong men. Her past relationships were made up of constant arguing, breaking up only to get back together, or simply doing off-the-wall things to make the other jealous. It was not only childish but exhausting.

"You never told me what had you flying in today?" Piper asked, continuing to measure her steps. Walking at this slow pace was so annoying, but it did give her time with Scott, so the trade-off was fair.

"I am a computer technician and work for a company in Milwaukee, Wisconsin. Although I live in Atlanta, I'm only here one week out of the month because of my schedule."

"That sounds like fun. Because I love traveling, I mean."

"Some days it is, other days not so much. Hard to catch your footing when you do a lot of moving around."

"I imagine so."

They finally arrived in front of the Souvenir Shop, and Piper shuffled her way in. The girl behind the counter gave them an odd look before speaking.

"Welcome to Remembered Souvenirs. Can I help you find anything?"

"Do you have any leggings?"

"Yes, over to the left near the sweatshirts."

Piper was so relieved she almost jumped for joy. She and Scott walked over to the limited supply of clothes. It was next to a shelf of pens, mugs, and 'I love Atlanta' picture frames.

There were only three choices. One was all black, another was blue, and the last one had the Atlanta Falcons logo plastered all over it. Picking up the one biased to the home football team Scott offered it to her.

"You should get these."

Piper made a face.

"Why?"

"Why not? Don't you love your Falcons?"

"I'm not into sports, actually."

"Blasphemy!" Scott said, feigning shock. "Who doesn't like sports?"

"This girl."

Piper picked up the black pair instead.

"But I'd love to see you in them," Scott said.

Smiling, she asked, "Who says you'll see me in them? I may take my leggings and mysteriously disappear."

"Don't be that way. A guy can hope to see a beautiful girl in leggings that represent his favorite sport can't he?"

"He can, but I like the black leggings better."

She turned towards the register and felt a gentle hand on her shoulder.

"Please. I bet you'd look so sexy in them, and I'll even pay for it," he said, offering the leggings again.

She faced him. He had such a charming way about him and soulful eyes.

"I don't need you to pay for it. You already saved me from public nudity. You've done enough."

"Think of it as a gift from a friend."

"Oh, so we're friends now?" Piper asked, biting her lip.

"For now. Eventually, we could be more."

There was that smile again. So damn sexy she could feel it in her toes. It made her want to cancel her babysitting plans and huddle up in a corner with him like a schoolgirl skipping class. Piper considered his request. One thing was for sure, Scott Bolden made it difficult for a girl to say no.

The problem was, Piper wasn't good at accepting help from others, specifically monetary assistance. Borrowing money or getting gifts at random always made her feel strange, even when she was a little girl. The no-strings-attached gesture always seemed to resurface with so many strings Piper felt like a puppet.

"I'll tell you what, as a way to thank you for helping me, I'll get the ones you like, but I'll pay for them myself."

Placing the black ones back on the shelf and taking the other from his hand, she headed to the register. After making the purchase and changing into the leggings, he walked her to baggage claim, where she located her small, pink, and black rolling suitcase.

"Don't you have baggage to claim?" Piper asked.

He adjusted the black book bag with blue letters on his shoulder.

"Nope, this is it. Since I practically live here and there, I don't need to bring much coming or going."

"Oh, that makes sense."

They watched each other for a moment longer, and then Piper extended her hand.

"I guess this is where we say goodbye."

He took her hand and kissed it. Piper felt warm all over.

"This could be where we say goodbye unless . . . " his lips quirked up into a grin.

"Unless what?"

Scott nodded in the direction of the little newsstand store with three sets of tables and chairs located on the outside.

"Would you have coffee with me?"

Piper looked down at her watch and begin to shake her head.

Noticing her about to object, he added, "Just for a few minutes."

She pulled her cell from her purse to check the time and noticed several missed calls and texts. They were likely from her best friend wanting to make sure Piper had safely landed. According to the time, it would be cutting it close, but she could spare ten more minutes before leaving was a must.

"Coffee sounds nice."

Scott ordered a coffee with no cream or sugar, and Piper settled for a bottle of water. They chose one of the three vacant tables, and Piper quickly sent off a text to her friend, confirming that aliens hadn't captured her . . . this time, and then looked up at Scott.

"That has to be gross. No sugar or cream. Who does that?"

"Crazy people, maybe?" he answered with a sly grin.

"I can believe that."

He took a sip and then leaned back into his chair.

"Are you single?"

"Yes, what about you?" she asked, suspecting he was.

"I am. Honestly, I haven't dated in a while."

"Why's that?"

He looked down and was quiet so long she thought he wasn't going to answer the question.

"My wife died a year ago. Now it's just my little guy, Ryan and I."

"That's horrible. I am so very sorry. What happened, if you don't mind me asking?"

"A car accident."

Piper touched her chest, and then before she knew it, his hand, offering comfort at his unfortunate loss.

He looked up with a pitying smile.

"I don't like to talk about it, especially since Ryan was only a month old when it happened. Now, he's thirteen months and never got the chance to know his mother."

Speaking about death was all too familiar for Piper in that instance. It was the other part of the reason, or rather the main reason a trip to Miami was necessary at all. Her Aunt Delores, who had practically raised her, or tried to when Piper wasn't being a stubborn teenager, was dying. Her aunt had severe diabetes that was affecting her health at an alarming rate.

"I understand more than you know," Piper commented quietly.

"Yeah, it's rough, but I make it through. The saddest part is work keeps me so busy. I had to hire a nanny to take care of Ryan when I'm not there."

The sincerity and guilt in his eyes caused her to feel deep pangs of sadness on his account.

"But I'm sure you're doing the best you can."

He nodded his agreement.

"It also helps that Simone, she's my live-in nanny, is great with Ryan."

"Oh wow, a live-in nanny. Is that expensive?"

"It could be, but Simone is in college studying to be a nurse. She gets free room and board for the three weeks while I'm working, and then the week I'm home, she stays with family or something while I spend time with Ryan. I also pay her a small amount for the help out."

"You've got a good thing going there."

"I miss Ryan like crazy, but it works out. Between Simone and daycare, I don't think he notices I'm gone. He has a pretty busy schedule."

Scott's phone rang, and he spared a glance at it before silencing it.

"Sorry, it's work. They call a lot."

She gestured to the black bookbag, propped up next to his chair. The words 'Lancer Communications' were printed diagonally in bold, blue square letters.

"Is that the company you work for?"

He looked down at the bag.

"That's them. I work all these odd hours setting up and making computer repairs at all their different locations. A lot of days, I may start at 6 am and not finish until 2 am."

"You are busy."

"I have a lot of bills. Handling everything alone is expensive, but it's worth it. I work non-stop for three weeks, and then I get a full week off." He shrugged. "Fair enough."

"How long have you worked for them?"

"Lets' see, I've worked for the company for five years, but this traveling position I only recently started."

"Why don't you simply relocate there? I mean so you wouldn't have to move around so much."

"Ryan mostly. My late wife, Julia's parents, are still alive, and I wouldn't want to take Ryan away from them."

Piper nodded in understanding.

"Of course, doing what's right for your son."

She already admired his dedication as a father. If possible, it made him that much more attractive to her.

"What about your family?"

"I'm an only child, and my parents died some time ago."

He looked away, uninterested in speaking any further on that topic Piper sensed. She decided to change the subject.

"I assume you have a place in Milwaukee?"

"Barely. I rent an apartment so small the kitchen and bathroom practically share a space. Management keeps telling me that in the next year, a position should open up in Georgia, and my days of traveling for work will be over."

He silenced his ringing cell again.

"Anyway, enough about me, tell me more about your job, or shall I say jobs?"

"Alright, the stripping I've done for four years now. A year and a half into it, I decided I wanted a college degree, so I continued to work at the club while I went to school. I graduated last year, and eight months ago, I got a job at a veterinary clinic. I work there Monday through Friday during the day, and I strip on the weekends."

"Whoa. You have a full plate, and also, congratulations."

"Thank you," she said, being reminded of how proud she was of herself.

"You said you're going to stop stripping. When is that?"

"In three weeks, I'll be done."

"I guess I better get by there fast?"

"That would be wise. I work at the Golden Bar."

Piper rechecked the time. The ten minutes were up.

She stood and collected her things.

"Gotta go, Scott."

"Wait," he said, standing as well. "I'd like to see you again. Can I at least have your number?"

Piper walked over and kissed him on the cheek.

"If you want me. You know where to find me," she said before walking away.

"Where in the hell have you been? I needed to know you landed safely. What if you got kidnapped?" Piper's best friend, Alisha Stein, aka Lish, said a little too loud in her ear.

"Lish, if that happened, they'd return me because they would get tired of my phone ringing with calls from you."

Piper got her suitcase out of her trunk and entered her apartment building, deciding first to check her mailbox since she hadn't been home in four days.

"Don't be sassy with me. You are the second sexiest woman on this earth. Somebody might want you all to themselves."

"The second?"

"Duh, you know I'm the first."

Piper laughed and did a quick flip through the envelopes addressed to her. Most were junk mail; the others were bills. Shoving the mail into her purse, she grabbed her suitcase and headed to the stairs. The elevator would have been easier, but she only lived on the second floor, and the luggage wasn't heavy. Not to mention, cutting corners wouldn't keep her body in shape.

"I'll keep that in mind. Sorry I didn't respond as soon as I landed. I intended to but got sidetracked."

"Sidetracked?"

Piper could practically see Lish's ears perk up at the word.

"To sum it up, I lost my skirt and met a guy."

"Now this sounds popcorn worthy, and it makes up for you missing my calls. Please continue."

"You know the beautiful floral skirt that I had to have when we went shopping last month?"

"Yeah."

"It got caught in an escalator and practically ripped from my body."

"Oh shit, you showed the goods to people roaming the airport? You naughty girl! I knew you weren't ready to stop stripping."

"Trust me, I am. Luckily for me, at the last second, a very handsome gentleman saved the day."

"Please tell me that I'm invited to the wedding?"

Piper rolled her eyes and gave her friend the sarcastic answer she always did.

"Yes, Lish. You're invited to the wedding, and I'll make sure you get the bouquet."

"That's why I love you."

"I love you, too."

"By the way, how is Aunt Delores?"

"Not great, but hanging in there. She told me she was in a lot of pain. I mostly just sat with her and talked. I went to the beach once, but it wasn't very enjoyable. Russell was glad I came down too."

Russell was Piper's cousin and her aunt's only child.

"You know I'm there for you if you need anything, right?"

"Yes! You don't have to keep telling me that. Let's talk about something else, though. Are you going to work tonight?"

"I am indeed. People want to see pussy, and I want to see payments. Therefore, the cat lady and I will be front and center stage."

Lish was 28 years old and loved being a stripper. She'd been "sliding down the pole", as she called it, for seven years and told Piper she didn't plan on quitting until either her pussy fell off or they put her out. She loved the money, the attention, and the adrenaline.

"Well, you and cat lady enjoy your night. I'm about to climb these stairs. Talk to you tomorrow, ok?"

"Sure thing."

She dropped the phone into her purse, picked up the suitcase, and started the climb to the second floor.

Piper lived in 2A, and overall, it was peaceful. The building itself was nice, and so were most of the residents. There were no significant issues, well, unless you counted those living in apartments 2B and 2C. Apartment 2D was currently vacant.

2B was a freaky couple named Lacy and Vince who had sex more than Piper thought humanly possible. If that wasn't enough, they were into some of the most bizarre things she'd ever heard of. Nipple clamps that you plugged into outlets, chain outfits for men and women, and even flavored fruit baskets that you soaked your feet in for your partner to lick off.

Piper tuned in every chance she got to their strange sex sessions, which wasn't hard to do because they could be heard going at it through her bedroom wall a lot of the time. To date, Piper hadn't witnessed any of the gadgets being used firsthand, but between what she could hear and from what they told her during their short chats while picking up the mail, she got the gist. Every time they got hot and heavy, Piper promised herself that she wouldn't listen in, but curiosity always won out.

As far as Leo went, the man in 2C, his only problem was that everyone in the building hated him, which was fair because he hated everyone.

Lugging her suitcase upstairs, Piper stopped twice to catch her breath.

"Damn it. I should have taken the elevator," she said.

Continuing to ascend one slow step at a time, Piper finally arrived at the top. Straightening her back and placing the suitcase down on its wheels, she walked to her front door, unlocked it, and pushed the door open.

"Home sweet home," she said aloud and then screamed in horror.

CHAPTER 2

Beating her into her own place at a speed that was both impressive and terrifying was a lizard.

Piper rushed inside, abandoning her purse and suitcase right beyond the entryway. A few steps in, and she almost broke her neck, tripping over unopened delivery boxes she'd left on the floor before her trip.

Spotting the greenish-brown, slimy-looking creature, she cursed. The lizard may have been small, but those powerful legs would make it exceptionally talented at evading capture. Then, out of nowhere, the worst thing happened. Speedy legs decided to dash from the sink area over to the kitchen island.

Its new location of choice was a brilliant score for him and a brand new issue for her. Piper's kitchen island was light-colored granite at the top, but the bottom was a deep woodsy brown. At least by the sink, it was easily visible. Now she would need a flashlight to find him.

"You just had to have the apartment with the island, didn't you, Piper?"

Of course, when she first saw it, she thought it was so cute; obviously, the lizard felt the same.

Torn between going back to her purse for her phone to use the flashlight feature or keep going forward to not risk losing the lizard, a sudden decision snapped into place. Losing track of it would be worse, so she pressed ahead.

Stepping closer to the island, Piper stopped to say a quick prayer that the lizard wouldn't rush out at her. If it did, she'd be likely to leave it the entire apartment, furniture included.

With eyes glued to the dark trim at the base of the island, she saw a tiny tail wiggle. It made her jump back and squeal, then bumping into someone caused her to yelp again.

"Daya! You scared me!"

"I scared you?" Daya questioned in disbelief. "I come over to drop off Jake, and the door is wide open, and you're moving like a ninja across the kitchen."

"You could have called my name."

"I didn't know what I was walking into! What's going on?"

"Ugh, a lizard got in, and I'm trying to get him out."

At that instant, Piper realized she had no plan. What did she think she could do? Point to the exit, and it would scurry out quickly and quietly?

"Maybe you can trap it in something? Or use bug spray on it? That may help, right?" Daya offered.

"I highly doubt bug spray would work for a lizard."

"If you use enough of it, it probably will."

In that instant, Jake ran inside, filling the room with his 4-year-old energy and wonderment at the mention of the lizard.

"A lizard. Let me see! Let me see!" He exclaimed.

"Jake, I told you to wait outside until I called you."

"But why Mom? Everything is fine, Miss Piper is fine, the apartment is fine. I want to see the lizard."

"That's not the point."

"What is the point?"

Daya looked up to the ceiling. It was clear Jake was tapping on her last nerve.

"You know what, Jake?" Piper said, a brilliant idea forming in her head. "If you can catch it. I will give you $5."

Jake's eyes nearly fell out of his head.

"A whole $5?"

"Yup."

Jake faced his mom with pleading eyes.

"Can I please?"

Daya shrugged.

"I don't care. You won't catch it anyway."

Jake was not discouraged even the slightest by his mom's non-existent faith in his abilities. He was ready for the challenge. Piper gave him a plastic bowl with a lid and pointed to the area where she last saw the unwanted guest.

She could only hope that it hadn't run off to tour more of her apartment during the brief conversation with Daya. Thankfully, the lizard was where she had last seen it, and, as Jake approached, it hurried across the kitchen towards a chair in the living room.

Piper and Daya gasped, relocated to stand on a couch opposite the chair, and grabbed hold of each other while Jake ran after it getting on all fours to peer under the sofa. Creeped out by Jake's nearness, it zigged zagged from one corner of her apartment and then to the other.

The boy nearly caught it as it rounded another chair, but it ran the opposite way at the last second. At one point, Jake tripped over one of Piper's boxes but didn't miss a beat, getting up and charging forward once again.

He was giving all the attention to catching the lizard and none to his surroundings. His next accident happened when he knocked over a small crystal mermaid statue she had near the edge of the coffee table. It shattered into what looked like a million tiny pieces, and Jake froze in his tracks.

He must have been about to apologize, but Piper waved him on. The lizard was getting away, and although she liked that mermaid, she loved a lizard-free apartment more.

After what seemed like forever, Jake got the lizard to surrender. He didn't catch it but annoyed the hell out of it. After performing one final sprint around the apartment, it exited through the still-open front door.

"Thank you so much, Jake. You almost destroyed my house, but you did a great job."

At hearing her appreciation, his shoulders slumped, and his eyes dropped to the ground.

"But I didn't catch it."

She placed an arm around his shoulder and pulled him close.

"But you earned five bucks."

"You're still going to pay me?"

"I am because without you, I would have had to move out of my apartment."

She collected $5 from her purse and presented it to him.

He stared at it and then went into overdrive on all the things he could buy with it. After stating he could purchase two bikes, Daya shook her head and sent him to the living room to watch TV.

"That boy has no idea that $5 can't buy half of that stuff."

"He'll learn," Piper said.

"Sooner than I'd like," Daya sighed. "He's growing up so fast. Either way, it's been fun, and now I'm late for work."

"Sorry," Piper winced.

Daya held up a hand. "No, it's fine. This is more action than I get down at the bar." She turned to Jake, absorbed in a show in the living room, and spoke louder. "You know the rules. Listen to Ms. Piper, don't be noisy and . . . "

"Eat all my food. I know, Mom. I'm not a little kid."

Daya faced Piper, "You can keep him, if you want. He has a smart mouth, but he's good for getting into tiny spots."

Piper laughed, spun Daya around by the shoulders, and said, "Bye, get to work. I'll see you at ten."

Daya waved goodbye and pulled up the door behind her. She was a cool girl—only 22, a single mom, and doing the best she could to take care of her son. One evening a week, Piper kept Jake so that Daya could work an extra shift.

So far, Piper had been doing this for the last five months, and she didn't see an end in sight. But she didn't mind helping out because Daya was a hard worker and a good person. Plus, Jake was hilarious, inquisitive, and a true ball of energy.

"Alright, Jake, are you good for a minute? I need to unpack."

"Jake," she repeated when he didn't answer. This time she clapped her hands when she called his name.

"I said okay," he answered.

He hadn't said anything unless he meant to himself, but debating that was pointless. Instead, Piper saved her energy for unpacking her clothes.

She pulled the suitcase into her room and unzipped it. The neatly packed bag she took with her was replaced by the messiness of what happens when you shove everything inside last minute to avoid missing your flight.

Dumping all the worn clothes into a laundry basket, an image of the beautiful Miami ocean popped into her mind. It had been so calming and serene, but she was unable to rely on its majestic blue waves as a dependable escape. Her aunt was dying, and nothing would change that.

When Piper was 14 years old, Aunt Delores took Piper in to live with her and her only son, Russell, who was 19 at the time. Piper's mother, Colleen Drummers, was never interested in having, let alone raising a child, and made that fact apparent.

Piper's dad, Alex Fosters, was a kind man, who loved Piper very much, or so she was told because Piper barely remembered him. He was killed in a convenience store robbery when she was four.

After he died, the full parenting responsibility fell on her mother's lap, and as expected, that didn't work out so well. She wasn't cruel or abusive to Piper, but she often pawned her off on family members for long periods without leaving any contact information or her whereabouts. Eventually, Colleen's older sister, Delores, took Piper in.

The good news was that Piper gained a stable home, but unfortunately, being overlooked for so long made her feel invisible. But instead of shying away from all things, she did her best to get noticed.

Causing trouble, dating all the wrong guys, getting several tattoos, and even becoming a stripper to add shock value. All of her aunt's attempts to prove to Piper that she was loved, special, and wanted seemed to fall on deaf ears. That younger version of Piper was angry, confused, and unknowingly carrying around a great deal of hurt.

She hadn't seen or heard from her mother since the day her aunt took her in. The voices of question in her head throughout the years constantly tugged at her. If her own mother could discard her so easily, wouldn't everyone else?

Piper's mindset changed when she turned 22 and had to spend a weekend in jail due to being at the wrong place, at the wrong time, with the wrong people.

That weekend gave her the ability to discern between the truth and the lies. There was nothing like a small room, with iron bars filled with silence to get you thinking. The endless pleading her aunt had done with her to make better choices were now pouring in, and for the first time, Piper understood.

Whatever her mother's issues were, they belonged to her mother, not Piper. It was her life to do with it as she pleased, and nothing was standing in her way. Her dreams, hopes, and goals could be achieved if she worked her ass off and stopped feeling sorry for herself.

Aunt Delores was thrilled with Piper's sudden enthusiasm to change. In addition, she pushed for Piper to give up stripping, but that was one thing Piper wasn't hearing.

Not only did she enjoy her job and the attention, but the money would also be beneficial in helping her pay off school debts while attending so that on graduation day, she owed no one.

Reluctantly her aunt accepted the decision, on the condition that when school was over, Piper would give up her X-rated nightlife career for a more professional, 'respectable' day job.

Piper stopped putting away items from her suitcase and looked at her reflection in the bedroom mirror. Eyes identical to her mother's stared back at her. It would be nice to share all that she'd achieved with her mom, but that was never going to happen. At least, her aunt was proud of her, and most importantly, she was proud of herself.

The trip had been good. Sad but good. Her aunt wouldn't leave this earth without knowing that she meant the world to Piper. The only regret was that it took Piper so long to recognize that, but one couldn't change their past, only their future, and her future looked pretty good. And now that she'd met Scott, it looked pretty *damn* good.

The look in his eyes made her feel like the only woman in the world. Until now, she never knew statements like that were true. There was no doubt that he would show up at the club. If he didn't, it simply wasn't meant to be, but he would, so there were no worries.

Piper jumped when her cell phone buzzed. That damn lizard still had her on edge. The display read, 'Chloe' and Piper sent it to voicemail.

Chloe was her cousin, on her father's side, and a person she genuinely adored. Her childhood afforded her a lot of time with various cousins, and she quickly decided which ones she loved and which she hated. The latter was the reason she silenced the phone.

Chloe was calling yet again to ask her to attend a fashion party at her twin cousins, Talia and Tina's house. They had launched a clothing line and wanted to celebrate by show-casing their designs.

Piper loved to shop, which meant being first in line to attend this event made sense, but the issue was Piper couldn't stand Tina. The reasoning was simple, really—Tina was a bitch.

Ever since they were kids, Tina thought that everyone should kiss her ass. For the most part, it worked because she was the popular girl in school. If she liked you, you were approved; if she didn't, you watched from the sidelines.

As the girls aged, improvements in their relationship should have set in due to maturity, but they didn't. Instead, it got worse, specifically when Tina heard about Piper becoming a stripper. Every time Piper came around, a rude comment broadcasting Tina's disgust awaited her.

So, it was shocking when Tina suddenly apologized for her actions a couple of years ago. Nevertheless, Piper refused to believe any of it. Tina was vindictive; her apology must have had an angle.

However, Tina's sister Talia was sweet and had never done anything wrong to Piper. They may have been twins, but their personalities were night and day. Talia was the only reason Piper was even considering going to that party. Talia deserved support and an in-person congratulations, not some card sent through the mail.

On the one hand, she only had three weekends left to work at the club. Attending this party would occupy one of those Saturdays and cut into her plans for saving a little more money before letting it go for good. Then again, it would also be nice to see her cousin Chloe again. It had been a while since they hung out, and Piper did miss her.

The text indicator chimed, and she picked it up and laughed.

Chloe: I know you're ignoring my call because you don't want to tell me you're not going to the party.

Piper: You know me so well.

Chloe: Don't be that way, it'll be fun.

Piper: With Tina there? I doubt it.

Chloe: Come on Piper. Some people take longer to grow, but Tina has done a lot of growing.

Piper: I'm still not convinced.

Chloe: Will you come for me? I haven't seen you since the BBQ where you met Reggie, and now we're married. It's been way too long.

Chloe had a point, and it made Piper feel bad. They not only got along but lived in the same state. It made no sense that they hardly saw each other.

Piper: Alright. I will seriously consider it and get back to you later.

Chloe's reply showcased her appreciation in numerous happy emojis, and the chances of Piper attending increased a few notches.

"Hi-yah!" Jake yelled from the living room.

He was watching the karate cartoon he loved. That kid was obsessed with dinosaurs and kicking. Once, when they were play fighting, one of his blows landed on her leg, causing her to limp for a week. No more karate matches for her.

Now that the unpacking was complete, it was time to prepare dinner. Piper wasn't big on cooking and suspected it was because she didn't know how to. The thought was dreadful.

Her specialty was fast food, microwave dinners, and anything that could be tossed in the oven, already seasoned and portioned. Learning to cook meals beyond hotdogs, french fries, and hamburgers was a definite necessity for the future of her arteries.

Yet, the inspiration to learn hadn't really struck. To force the desire, a few months back, she purchased kitchen gadgets such as a rice cooker, air fryer, wok, food slicer, etc., but they were still boxed up in her cabinets, collecting dust.

After searching the freezer, she located a box of hamburger patties.

"Hamburgers it is," she said, pulling out the familiar meal.

"Hey, Miss Piper, how old are you?"

Piper placed her hands on her hips.

"Why?" she said suspiciously, lifting an eyebrow.

"Just want to know."

"A girl never reveals her age, but I can tell you this, I'm old enough."

"Old enough for what?"

"Movies without color and landline phones," she replied, teasing him.

"What's a landline?" he asked, abandoning the show to face her.

"It's a phone that calls people just like a cell, but it has to be plugged into the wall."

"Oh," he said, satisfied with the answer. A few seconds later, he had another question for her.

"What were dinosaurs like?"

Piper laughed out loud.

"Jake, I wasn't around when dinosaurs were here."

"But I thought you said you were old enough?"

"Not that old! Just how old do you think I am?"

"I don't know," he said, shrugging, "like a hundred."

That was enough to prompt her to share.

"Jake, I'm 26. Not 100."

"That's almost the same thing, isn't it?"

Piper shook her head and popped the hamburgers in the oven. Her mood had lifted. She'd met a fantastic guy, was now living in a lizard-free apartment, and had the company of a handsome yet although adorably insulting four-year-old for dinner. Things were good. So good that she would take Chloe's advice and go to the party.

CHAPTER 3

The dog barked and barked and barked. He had been barking all morning, and now Piper was starting to get a headache. The dog's name was Thunderbolt, and Piper felt horrible for the little guy. He was pissed about being locked in a cage. According to her boss, he had separation anxiety. Still, even though she understood his complaints, it was hard to do her job when he wouldn't stop barking.

Already, Maxine Stern's invoice was printed twice. The first time Piper had mistakenly left the 'S' off of Stern. The second time, she got the name right but forgot to re-add the date. There was even almost a third mess up when she caught herself putting it in the collections folder instead of the outgoing mail folder where it belonged.

One would think that by now, after working at a veterinarian clinic for eight months, she would have learned to concentrate through all the pet-created noise; however, they would be wrong.

Not only was her office too close to all the clinic's

unhappy guests, but staying up all night watching her favorite medical dramas on TV was also a poor decision.

She'd promised herself that after an hour, showtime would be over. Somehow one hour turned into five without her consent. The TV simply drew her in, and it would be rude to stop watching mid-show or mid-season, for that matter.

Today was Friday, and even with little sleep, surviving the shift should have been a piece of cake. Except, she'd forgotten about the noise and was now paying for it dearly.

The clock readout displayed 9 am. The workday ended at 3 pm, and already, it felt like she'd been there long enough to do her shift twice.

When she first started working at Granted House Veterinarian Clinic, she felt accomplished and ready to apply all the skills taught during college. The owner, an older woman in her sixties, named Mrs. Friedman, seemed eager too. The position needed to be filled, and she pointed out how much she liked Piper's spunk.

That wasn't a word Piper had ever heard anyone use in real life, but she smiled and graciously accepted the compliment since it came with a job offer. The pay wasn't excellent, but it was her first job out of college, and Mrs. Friedman assured her that after a 90-day probationary period, if everything looked good, the pay would increase.

The 90 days had come, and Piper got the increase, but it was so small it barely made any difference in her paycheck. When Piper questioned her boss about it, the response was to promise another raise in six months.

Piper knew exactly what that meant. Mrs. Friedman was selling her a plate of bullshit. Nevertheless, what could she do?

Quitting abruptly wouldn't be professional and only serve as a major setback in her plan. She'd promised herself and her aunt that she would create a new life, and no matter the struggle or how manipulative the employer, she would do just that.

As easily as this job had been found, there had to be others. For now, Piper would remain at the clinic for at least a year to get the experience and a good reference, then move on.

Finally getting Mrs. Stern's bill correct, Piper went on to the next account. The amounts that people paid for their pet's medical expenses were insane. Never having owned a pet herself, Piper assumed that medical care for pets was less costly than what you paid for a human, but that was highly inaccurate.

After entering the details of the next five customer accounts, Mrs. Friedman approached her desk with a big smile on her face.

"How's your Friday going?"

What the fuck do you want? Piper thought.

It wasn't that she disliked the lady. Her manipulative tendencies aside, she was decent to work for. Still, every time she came to Piper with that smile, a request was close behind.

"Pretty good. What about yours?"

"It's great. All the owners are happy, and the animals are doing wonderful," she paused, listening to a barking Thunderbolt, "well, all of them are happy except one, but you can't win them all."

"Very true," Piper commented.

"Listen, would you mind giving us a hand cleaning the dog cages after lunch? I know it's not in your job description, but I would really appreciate it. You can even take an additional 30 minutes for lunch as an expression of my gratitude."

There it was. Mrs. Friedman wanted something. Piper

had already helped with the cages several times since she had worked there. Supposedly, Mrs. Friedman was going to hire someone to help out full-time since she and Dennis (another Veterinarian that helped out) couldn't handle all the tasks. Still, there was always an excuse why she hadn't done it.

I want to keep my job. I want to keep my job. Piper mentally reminded herself before opening her mouth to respond.

"Sure. I wouldn't mind helping out after my break."

"Splendid. The cleaning supplies are where they always are, and don't forget to scoop the poop," she added, a little too cheery as she spun and walked away.

Piper rolled her eyes and hit the keys on the computer much harder than intended. The whole time, her mind kept replaying releasing Thunderbolt from his cage so he could take a nice bite out of Mrs. Friedman's ass.

A little over six hours later, Piper arrived home tired of shit from the clinic, both literally and figuratively. Entering her apartment building, she performed the usual end of the workday rituals—checked the mail, and went into her apartment to strip. When alone, her outfit of choice was a T-shirt and underwear.

Being fully nude would have been preferable, but her phobia about the apartment building having an emergency evacuation where her only option would be to exit the building naked made her choose clothes every time.

Unboxing a microwave dinner and setting the timer for three minutes, she considered her next activity of the evening. Learning how to cook should have been on the list but never ranked high enough. Instead, she went to the TV and turned it on. It was time to start a new season of the medical dramas that caused her to lose sleep for work.

Damn, it was only 4:15 on a Friday afternoon, and instead of living like she was 26, her life closer resembled someone that was 62. The come home from work, turn on the TV and barely go out had unknowingly become her new normal.

Before college, most days, she was only home long enough to shower and change her clothes. Partying, shopping, and her shift at The Golden Bar was the fast-paced life she lived and loved.

However, after enrollment, life took a more mature turn. If she was going to pass her classes, she needed to study and work hard. Her days were dedicated to studying and attending classes and her nights to earning a living.

Once she graduated last year and cut down her shifts at the club to weekends only, her new position at the veterinarian clinic occupied her weekdays. Then she began watching Jake one evening out of the week for Daya, and there was officially no time for anything else.

When she was done working at the club in a few weeks, there may be an opportunity to restart her social life. The microwave dinged, indicating the meal was done. Piper removed it and placed it on the counter, allowing it to cool a little before digging in.

While waiting, now was a good time to text her cousin, Russell, and check on her aunt. Texting her aunt directly would have been easier, but she did a lot of sleeping these days; running the risk of waking her was unnecessary.

Russell's reply was instant and not encouraging. Aunt Delores was still in pain, still weak, and ready for it all to be over. In response, she sent her love and promised to call the next day.

Collecting her food tray and a bottle of water from the kitchen, Piper sat down in front of the couch and turned up the volume. She needed a break from her own drama, and what better way to escape your own than to dive into someone else's.

Piper was going to be late; it was Saturday evening, and she was rushing to get to her wax appointment before her shift at the club.

"Stiletto heels, check. Skimpy outfits, check. Nail polish, check. But where is my body glitter spray?"

Lifting a box of shoes in her closet to ensure it hadn't fallen off the shelf, she suddenly recalled that it was in the fridge.

One of the dancers told her it sticks better to the skin if stored at a cooler temperature. Piper had no idea if it were true, but it was worth a try. Grabbing the spray out of the refrigerator door, Piper did one final check before leaving the apartment and heading to her wax appointment.

The appointments were every five weeks, like clockwork. Today's service fell on a work night, so tonight's crowd would be lucky enough to enjoy a freshly waxed treat. Driving the fifteen minutes it took to get to the Waxing Spa, Piper signed in and took a seat while waiting for Olga, her usual waxer, to call her back.

Sitting there, Piper recalled her very first waxing experience. It happened shortly after becoming a stripper. Piper met the woman who had now become her best friend.

Lish was funny, bold, sexy, and insistent that waxing was a must. As a new dancer who only hoped to one day earn as much as Lish did, who was Piper to disagree with her? Therefore, a few days later, Piper set up her first appointment.

Before making it to the table, she felt anxious. Stripping was one thing but having a strange woman closely inspecting her lady business felt weird. Even still, turning back was not an option, so she settled in for the quick hair removal process.

Her initial thought was that it wouldn't be as painful as people on TV made it seem. Those scenes must have been exaggerated, or people had a low threshold for pain. There was no way an action that was over with so quickly could cause such a reaction.

She was wrong in her assumption because, in her case, those scenes were understated. Piper was not at all ready for how painful and messy getting waxed was. She bled like a gutted fish on the table, and her entire vaginal region hurt for the next few hours.

Shuddering at the unpleasant recollection, she was pulled entirely from memory lane when Olga entered the waiting area and waved her back. The process barely took ten minutes, and Piper was out the door feeling smooth and sexy.

Pulling into a parking spot at The Golden Bar, she grabbed her small black duffle bag and exited the car. There weren't many people around because she had parked in the back like most dancers and staff members usually did.

Upon a quick scan of the parking lot, Lish's car wasn't in sight. Piper presumed that meant her friend didn't work tonight, and the thought bummed her out a little. Seeing Lish before a show always gave her an extra oomph on stage. Their quick girl chats were like pep talks for football players before a game.

As she neared the back door, a couple was blocking it with their arms wrapped around one another and mouths practically fused in a passionate kiss.

Neither of their faces were visible, but Piper suspected the woman was a dancer named Lily because there was a bunny tail glued to the ass of everything she wore.

"Excuse me," Piper said, clearing her throat.

The couple didn't stop their spit exchange for even a second.

"EXCUSE ME!" she said louder this time. They finally stopped kissing, and the girl turned around to glare at Piper.

"Oh, it's you," Lily said unbothered. "What do you want?"

"Isn't it obvious, Lily? You and your guy here are blocking the door."

That's when the guy leaned forward.

"Piper, baby, how are you?"

It was her ex-boyfriend, Quentin.

Piper rolled her eyes.

"I'm great, Quentin, and I see you are too. Can you and Lily please excuse me?"

"Of course, we can," Quentin responded, although he didn't move. "Have you missed me?"

She hadn't missed him one little bit. Their entire relationship was an ongoing chain of strong highs and intense lows, with the lows being the usual. They argued about everything, from why she didn't like to cook to why he thought it was okay to check out other women.

The sex was magnificent and served as the main reason she couldn't let go. She believed their passion in the bedroom was love when it was actually naive lust. It took three and a half years of back-and-forth fighting for Piper to realize that.

"Not at all, Quentin. But I am missing getting paid."

She made a motion with her hand that signaled for them to make way.

"Come on, baby, let's get out of the way of my jealous ex. I can tell she still wants me. I wouldn't want her to start a fight."

Lily sucked her teeth to express her disgust, and Quentin laughed.

Piper ignored him and his delusional thoughts. What she

wanted was for Quentin to disappear and to take his bunny-tailed girl with him.

He was right about one thing, though, if she were the old Piper, her response to his antics would be to do something petty and vengeful. Then play innocent to get him back to her place and prevent him from ending up in another girl's bed.

Looking back, she laughed at how childish that response was. At the time, she didn't understand that you couldn't keep someone that didn't want to be kept. Yup, their relationship was toxic, alright. Toxic, petty, and stupid. Thank God that was over.

Piper went inside and downstairs to her dressing area. She was due on stage in 30 minutes. That gave her enough time to do her makeup, paint her toenails and get dressed.

Finishing up with five minutes to spare, Piper put her items away in a corner locker, did one last check on her face, and went upstairs.

The stage she normally used was located to the left of the center stage. There was a total of five stages in the club, and at least three were always occupied.

All she needed to do was hit the top button on the side-wall, and the lights to her stage would flood on. Timing it as a new song began to overtake the one fading out, Piper hit the lights for her staging area before climbing the five stairs, which led to the thick double curtains, and right behind those lay the audience.

As soon as the curtains parted, she heard cheering and applause. Stepping forward, matching her movements to the beat, she waved flirtatiously to the crowd. She then grabbed onto the tall, thick golden pole.

Immediately she was in the zone, allowing the music to control her actions, overtake her thoughts, and dictate when to pull off articles of clothing. Her eyes were closed, and her body felt free.

The lacy, red, and blue glittered bra with bright red matching thongs was the first to go. Air from a vent above the stage hit her nipples just as she was arching back away from the pole and her tiny brown buds sprouted to attention.

She squeezed and played with each of them while licking her glossy, cherry-covered lips. Sliding down to the floor, Piper spread her legs wide and toyed with her panty line moving it slightly to the side only for a second to give the drooling audience a peak.

Whistles and shouts sprang out from all sides, and a feeling of invincibility flooded her. She continued teasing, playing, and showcasing her talents for another 20 or 30 minutes and then collected her clothes and tips and returned to the dressing room.

Taking ten minutes to change outfits and freshen up her makeup, Piper repeated the same process three more times before taking an official hour break.

A break from the heels, lights, and noise was necessary before completing her last four shows of the night. In total, she typically performed eight shows. However, that was sometimes cut short if someone requested a private show.

Piper made her way to the bar area and took a seat.

"I got your water coming right up, Piper," Sidney said.

Sidney had been the bartender at The Golden Bar for two years and knew what all the dancers liked to drink. She was sweet, professional, and had great breasts that really gave her a boost in tips.

"Thanks, Sidney."

"Why don't you let me buy you a drink?" came a familiar husky voice from behind her.

Piper exhaled and tried to ignore the comment. Without

turning around, she already knew it was Gus. A club regular who was mostly harmless but highly exasperating.

"No, Gus."

He coughed. It was a wet, gross sound, courtesy of the tobacco he constantly chewed. Gus placed a meaty palm on the bar next to her hand.

"You always say no. Why is that?"

She opened her mouth to respond but was cut off by another male voice on her opposite side.

"Because she was waiting for me."

The guy stepped into view, and schoolgirl giddiness and butterflies instantly replaced her displeasure.

"You came."

"You know I couldn't miss a chance at seeing you again. Your performance was amazing."

"I'm glad you liked it. Had I known you were in the crowd, I would have made it extra special."

He touched her face, and an irritated Gus stumbled away to find a new unlucky lady.

"How much longer do you work tonight?"

"I have four more shows. Why do you ask?"

"I was hoping to spend some time with you. I can wait until you're done."

She loved the idea of spending time with him. In fact, starting the evening right away sounded wonderful. Tomorrow night she had to work again. Leaving early tonight wouldn't be a huge deal. Besides, wasn't she just thinking she needed to have more fun?

"We can hang out now."

He looked surprised. "But don't you have to work?"

"I can leave early tonight."

He extended a hand. Taking it, she stood and smiled.

"Wait for me here," she said.

Returning to the dressing room, Piper collected her

things, changed into non-skimpy clothes, and met back up with Scott. He led her outside to his car, and she stopped when she saw the license plate.

"CasualT? That's um unique."

"I've always had a friendly, relaxed attitude, and in high school, I went by my middle name Thomas. Friends thought the nickname CasualT was fitting, so it stuck."

"Aww, that's cute. Maybe not best suited on the back of a car, but cute."

He chuckled.

"I give you my word Piper. I'm a safe driver. Speaking of where is your car?"

"It's in back. I don't mind riding with you, and you drop me back off here. We can go to a 24-hour diner up the street and talk."

"Works for me."

He opened the door for her and then slid into the driver's seat. It only took a total of two minutes to get there and another minute to be seated. It was 10:30 at night on a Saturday, so the place was mostly empty. Too late for the older crowd and too early for those seeking a decent spot for hangovers.

He stared at her from across the table.

"I'm so glad to see you. Would it be too soon to say I missed you?"

"Would it be too soon for me to say I feel the same?"

It was the truth. She had thought of him a lot, actually. The desire to see his face and feel his touch was never too far away in her mind. However, it wasn't until now that she understood how drawn she was to him. He had such warm eyes, and his presence made her feel energetic and alive.

He took her hand and didn't let go until their orders came. They spent several hours getting to know one another and sharing stories of their childhood, adult lives, and hobbies. He was an only child, born and raised in Denver. He loved computers, fishing, and spending time with his son.

His level-headedness was refreshing. She'd never dated a man that was so charming, professional, and stable. He listened intently to every word as she talked about her childhood and issues with her mom, gently interjecting only to comfort her with his touch and words.

The night was lovely, and neither of them wanted it to end, but Scott had to get back to his son, Ryan.

"I had a nice time, beautiful. Are you free anytime tomorrow?"

"I have to be back at work by eight tomorrow night, but I'm free before that."

"Tomorrow night, I head back to Milwaukee for another three weeks, so normally, I spend the day with my son. However, I'd like to see you before I go."

"That would be nice, but I don't want to take you away from Ryan."

"You're sweet," he said, gliding his thumb across her lower lip. "Would you mind hanging out tomorrow with Ryan and me? You can say no. I won't take offense."

"I'd enjoy that. What time were you thinking?"

"There's a fair in town. I could pick you up around one. I'll have to be gone by six anyway."

"Okay," she said, inching closer towards him. "I'll give you my address and phone number, and you can come and get me when you want me."

"Oh, I want you," he said.

Their lips met, and the fireworks began in a dizzying heat that caused her heart to flutter. The taste of his lips were intoxicating, and she couldn't get enough of it.

Yes, it was official. Scott Bolden was the man of her dreams.

The ride lifted Piper in the air and then back down again, making her stomach flip, and she felt like an excited kid having the time of her life. A few minutes later, the ride ended. It was the fair; after all, the rides didn't last that long, and this one she had ridden solo.

"How'd you like it?" Scott asked as Piper exited the ride called Doom Spinner.

"I made it out with my life and felt like a giant kid in the process. Super fun."

She put her arms around Scott and kissed him on the lips and then gave Scott's adorable, sweet baby boy, Ryan, a kiss on the cheek.

The day had been wonderful; not at all as challenging as Piper assumed a day at the fair with a one-year-old would be. True, it was a different type of date, but that's actually what she liked about it. The day was nice, lines were short, and they experienced all the suitable rides together, and the ones that they couldn't, they rode solo. Either Piper would hold Ryan for Scott to enjoy himself or vice versa.

Ryan reached for her, and she pulled him into her arms. Piper had never been around babies a lot, but she was already in love with this one. His chubby cheeks and big doe eyes pulled her in and wouldn't let go. Ryan gave her a juicy kiss on the cheek, and she beamed.

"Aww, you're the cutest too," she said, touching Ryan's nose and kissing him back.

"He takes to you really well, and he doesn't do that to everyone. I guess he knows a good woman when he sees her too, just like his dad," said Scott.

Piper blushed and bit her lip.

"I guess so."

Is this what it felt like to be a family? she wondered.

If it did, she could get with this, especially with Scott. He had been nothing but the perfect gentleman all day, complimenting her, holding her hand, giving her soft kisses on the forehead. She felt like the most beautiful woman in the world.

They decided to go grab a few snacks and drinks, so they headed to the food area before their next ride. They got in line behind two other people and checked the menu for the snacks they wanted to order.

"The funnel cake looks delicious," Piper suggested.

"I agree. We should get two. I love those. You want a slushy too. My treat?"

He had insisted on taking care of everything and pampering her all day, from paying for her parking to her food, games, and even a new shirt when Ryan threw up on her old one. The behavior of such gestures from guys was foreign to her. But protesting didn't work with Scott, so eventually, she gave in.

They stepped forward as one customer exited the line. As they awaited their turn, a woman walked over, stopped in front of them, and slapped Scott as hard as she could.

CHAPTER 4

"**W**HOA, WHOA," Scott shouted, grabbing the woman's hand just in time to avoid being struck a second time.

"Don't whoa whoa me, Garret! I'll bet you didn't expect to see me again."

"What the hell?" Piper said.

She cradled Ryan in her arms and took a step back to shield him from this unfolding drama. The few people standing around them stopped what they were doing and turned to see what all the commotion was.

"I think you have me confused," Scott said to the woman.

His voice sounded in control, firm, but soothing. Kudos to him because Piper would have retaliated first and asked questions later.

"I don't have you confused. I'm the one-night stand that woke up the next morning to you gone along with my grandmother's diamond ring that I kept on my nightstand."

She tried to lift the opposite hand, but Scott quickly blocked it as well; he was now holding one of her wrists in each of his hands.

"Listen, okay. What's your name?" he asked.

The woman rolled her eyes as she said, "Nicole. As if you didn't know."

"Alright, Nicole, just calm down. My name is Scott. Not Garret. I have never seen you before. But after what you've told me, I understand why you would be upset at this Garret guy. He sounds like a terrible person."

"You'd know. Since he… is you."

Nicole tried to pull her arm away, but Scott held firm. She then lifted a knee that Scott also successfully avoided.

Piper watched utterly speechless, not sure of what to say or what to do.

"Nicole," he said, still maintaining his comforting yet assertive tone. "I assure you. I am not him. My name is Scott Bolden and not only have I never seen you before. I am rarely even in this state."

For the first time, Nicole's expression changed as some of the hate left her eyes and her body relaxed.

"Okay," she said, eyeing him. "You look just like him, and you even sound like him. He had a tattoo on his left bicep of a motorcycle on fire."

Scott slowly released her wrists and held his palms up to keep her calm and hopefully from resorting back to attack mode. He took a step back from her and lifted his shirt sleeve, exposing his left bicep; there was no tattoo.

Nicole covered her mouth.

"Oh my goodness! I am so sorry. I just thought… I was sure… this is so embarrassing."

"It's fine, Nicole. They say everyone has a doppelgänger, and I guess mine happens to be an asshole."

The comment made Nicole laugh a little, and Piper watched in awe at how well Scott diffused such an intense situation. Ryan wiggled in her arms, and Piper tried to fight how turned on Scott's response to the crazy woman had made her.

Nicole squinted at Scott as she slowly said, "Come to think of it, his hair was different, and you are slimmer than he was. I'm so sorry again. I hope you have a good day."

"You as well," replied Scott.

Nicole gave both him and Piper one last apologetic smile and briskly walked away.

"Wow," Piper said once Nicole was gone, "that was weird and incredible."

"Yeah, I hope she finds the guy. Men like that are the lowest form of scum, but I wasn't going to let her ruin my perfect day with you."

"I can see that. Things could have easily gone south, but you handled it."

"I like to stay on top of things," he replied, taking her hand in his.

And I wonder how it would be if you were on top of me, Piper thought to herself.

"Hang from my balls, baby! Hang from my balls."

"Eww," Piper shrieked, leaning closer to the wall. Then suddenly backed away as she remembered that listening to Vince and Lacy's horror sex show was off-limits. It was immature, nosey, and an invasion of privacy, but it was so damn juicy that it was hard to control herself.

"That man is a whole circus act," Lish said.

Piper's sex-crazed neighbors, Vince and Lacy, were at it again. Vince was yelling the oddest statements while Lacy just yelled.

"I forgot what I was looking for," Piper said.

"The blue heels you said I could borrow."

"Oh yeah."

Piper went back to rummaging through her shoe collection for the requested heels, and Lish laid back onto the bed. The sounds of Vince's grunting and odd "come on's" still penetrated through the walls.

"All of the stuff he shouts out couldn't be real," Piper stated as she relocated two boxes of shoes and then a third, searching for a box with a blue top.

"I don't doubt it," Lish replied, studying her nails.

"Why not?"

"I told you about the time I slept with Vince, didn't I?"

Piper dropped the box she was holding and came over to sit down on the bed next to her friend.

"You did not!"

"Well, I did, and let me tell you that man is every bit as freaky and weird as he seems."

"Where was Lacy? No, better yet, where was I?"

"This was before he and Lacy got together, and you were out of town. At the time I came over, though, I had forgotten that you weren't there. Terry and I got into a fight, and I needed someplace to go, so I came to see you."

"Why didn't you go back home when I didn't answer? How did you end up at Vince's place?"

"An Uber brought me here, and I had been drinking, so I decided to stay put."

"You were going to sleep outside the door?" Piper asked, astonished.

"If I had to. I was not going back home to that asshole. Luckily Vince came out into the hall and invited me in."

"Uh-huh," Piper said, smiling and nodding.

"I had been drinking," Lish said, pointing a manicured finger at Piper. "So you can't judge me."

Piper held up her hands. "No judgments here. Only laughs."

"I was supposed to take this to my grave," Lish said, picking up a pillow and covering her face.

Piper pulled the pillow from her friend's hands.

"For this story, I'd harass you in your casket."

"Fine! Here's the short version. He offered me a drink, I took it, and then he took off his shirt and started doing push-ups.

Piper couldn't contain her laughter.

"Why did he do that?"

"Piper, it's Vince, who knows why he does anything. Either way, I don't know what was on my mind because he started looking good to me."

Piper gasped, and Lish held up a finger to avoid interruption.

"That tells you just how drunk I was. Next, he asked me if I wanted to touch his chest, and I said yeah. A couple of drinks later, we were in his bed getting it on."

"Wait, he didn't pressure you or anything, did he?"

"No, it wasn't like that. Everything was consensual. It just happened extremely fast."

"Gotcha."

"Alright, so we were going at it, and honestly, it was feeling good. Out of nowhere, I get the sensation of something sliding into my ass, and it was too large to be a finger."

Piper squinted.

"Your expression was identical to mine. Unless he had grown a second dick, something wasn't right."

"So, what was it?"

"It was a damn pickle with Vaseline on it!"

"Stop lying."

"I'm not! He must have pulled it from his nightstand or

something and just had it greased and ready because I swear I didn't see it when we got started."

Piper laughed so hard tears ran down her cheeks.

"But you were super drunk. It could have been there the whole time, and you wouldn't have noticed."

"You know what?" Lish said, thinking about it. "You're right. Still, don't judge me."

"Sorry, friend. I'm judging the fuck out of you right now," Piper replied through laughter.

Lish picked up the pillow and hit her with it. Piper continued to laugh, and Lish joined in.

"You've laughed enough at me now tell me about your date with Scott and his son."

"Oh, it was heavenly. We had so much fun, and his son is adorable. I hate that I don't get to see Scott for another three weeks."

"You can call him, though, right?"

"Yeah. I've spoken to him every day since he left on Sunday. Work keeps him very busy though, we can't always talk, but we at least text."

"That's nice. You seem happy."

"I am. He is sweet, thoughtful, and responsible. Nothing like Quentin."

"Good, because Quentin was a nightmare."

Piper nodded her agreement and walked back to the closet, restarting the search for the blue heels. As soon as she spotted them, her phone chimed. Picking it up, she smiled and read the message from Scott that said he was thinking of her and would call her later after work.

"That smiles looks like you're thinking naughty thoughts," Lish teased.

Piper bit her lip. Her mind was now entirely on Scott and that handsome face. At this point, she wanted him so bad naughty wasn't a dirty enough word.

Twindle. It was the word printed on the vast, bold, digital sign on the lawn. It was the name of the clothing company Piper's twin cousins Tina and Talia had launched.

The decor for this party was awe-inspiring. The twins had clearly gone all out, and it showed. As Piper entered the house, she saw that mannequins lined the living room walls, and others were on a stage. If that wasn't enough, live models paraded around in various outfits with signs on their back indicating which Twindle Collection the pieces came from.

The entire layout was well crafted, and the clothes were simply stunning. She could practically hear some of the shirts, jackets, and skirts begging to take up residence in her closet. One skirt, in particular, reminded her of the beautiful floral skirt the escalator had torn to shreds.

It was all worth it to meet Scott. Those soft lips, big hands, and—

"Piper, I'm going to go find Tina and Talia. You want to come with me?" her cousin Chloe asked from beside her.

"In a minute. Suddenly my mouth is dry. I need something to drink."

"We can go find drinks first."

"No, I'll catch up. You go ahead."

Chloe went to the right, and Piper continued walking straight ahead. She could see a table covered in appetizers and drinks.

Piper grabbed a bottle of water and two mini-size chocolate chip cookies. They were very soft and sweet she picking up a third and promised herself it would be the last. Piper took a moment to regard her surroundings.

In the corner of the room was another mannequin wearing a stylish blue and yellow wrap-around skirt. Next to that mannequin was another, wearing that same skirt, as a full dress. Piper instantly fell in love with the versatile garment.

Stepping closer to admire it, she spotted a small table with a clipboard and a sign that read, "do you want this item?"

Yes! She thought to herself.

Piper grabbed the clipboard and a pen and filled out a form. Towards the bottom of the sheet, a message stated the item would be delivered to the address provided within two to four weeks.

Scanning the form again, Piper noticed that there was no place to put payment information.

"Excuse me," she said, stopping one of the wait staff members that was carrying a tray of champagne. "Do you know how we provide payments for these items?"

"There is no charge. All of the items on display are free for the guests in attendance."

"Wow, that's nice," Piper said, taken aback.

The woman smiled and continued serving drinks.

After walking for around ten minutes, Piper caught up to Chloe. She was chatting with Talia, Tina, and another woman.

"Hi, Talia. Hi, Tina," Piper said.

"Pipes!" Talia said, calling her by a family-given nickname and hugging her.

Tina also hugged her, but it was less enthusiastic, and Piper didn't take offense. After all, the feeling was mutual.

"This is a gorgeous and creative party. I ordered a skirt and was told that all the items here are free. Are you guys crazy? I mean, I'll take it but aren't you in business to make money, not give it away?"

Chloe laughed.

"I asked them the same thing."

"You have to spend money to make money," Talia said. We

only invited our closest family and friends to this party, so giving away the items isn't breaking the bank. Plus, when all of you lovely guests wear these items out in public, people will ask where you got it from, and you will so kindly point them to our website."

"I gotcha, we are walking advertisements?"

"Exactly," Tina and Talia said collectively.

"That's a pretty good idea when you put it that way."

"Yeah, and if we do take a loss," Tina added, "it's no big deal. We are having another party next weekend, and for that one, the items will cost."

"I hope it works out. You both are very talented," Piper said.

"Thanks," both girls replied.

The evening continued to proceed with elegance and style. There was a fashion show at one point, and every item was a piece Piper would be thrilled to wear. She tried not to be too greedy and order everything, but keeping her love for clothes at bay was tough.

Before exiting the stage, the MC announced that there would be prize giveaways. Piper was floored. Wasn't this whole event a giveaway? Now there were prizes too.

Piper had to admit, it was fun, and the time with her cousin made it that much more special. She and Chloe danced, caught up on each other's lives, and even found matching outfits to order.

"Hey, Chloe, I'm going to grab another glass of champagne. You want one?"

"No, I'm fine. I'll be right here eyeing that sexy business suit over there?"

"You planning on ordering it?"

"No. I have ordered enough stuff," Chloe said unconvincingly.

Piper gave her a look.

"You're waiting until I leave to order it, aren't you?"

"Yes," Chloe said like an ashamed child.

Piper laughed and went to the drinks station.

Tina was standing on one end, talking to two other women, when Piper approached.

"One glass of champagne, please," she said to the bartender.

He nodded and grabbed a glass.

Her phone chimed with a message from Scott. She smiled.

Scott: Tied up with boring work stuff but wish I was with you.

Piper: I wish you were here too.

Scott: Call you soon, baby.

Piper slid the phone back into her purse just as the waiter placed the glass of champagne in front of her. Picking it up, she took a sip and savored the acidulous flavor.

"I don't like Kelly. She's so fake, and you know I can't stand fake people, " Piper overheard Tina say to the women.

Piper gave a sarcastic laugh much too loud and covered her mouth.

Oh Shit, she thought.

Tina looked in her direction, and Piper winced. The laugh really did slip out, but she doubted Tina would believe that.

"What's that, Piper?" Tina questioned, lifting a brow.

Piper shook her head and held up her hand.

"Nothing, it was nothing."

"Please, if you have something to say, don't let me stop you."

Piper put her drink down.

"I said it was nothing."

Tina rolled her eyes, and that pissed Piper off.

"Yeah, I do have something to say. Why is it that the fake people always call everyone else fake?"

The two women Tina was conversing with exchanged glances as their eyes widened.

"And who exactly would you be referring to when you say fake?" Tina asked in an elevated voice while putting her drink down.

Piper pretended to think and then said, "That would be you."

"I suggest you watch your mouth because you must have me mistaken."

"Mistaken for who?"

The two women stepped aside, and at that very moment, Chloe walked up.

"For someone who won't beat your ass," Tina said, heading in Piper's direction. At the same time, Piper began moving towards Tina.

Chloe rushed to jump in between her two cousins.

"Children, stop it. This is a party to celebrate and have a good time. We all love each other. There is no fighting here."

"I might love her, but I'll still put her in her place," Tina said, trying to get around Chloe.

"Try me," Piper spat back.

Both girls attempted to advance towards one another again, and Chloe used more force to maintain their separation.

"Stop this! Piper, come with me. Tina, go cool off."

"No need," Piper said. "I have a better idea. I'm going home."

"Smartest thing you've said all night," Tina mocked.

Piper walked past Chloe and Tina. Chloe called after her, but she didn't stop to respond. She felt angry for wasting her Saturday to come here and guilty that things had gotten out of hand much too fast. Before reaching her car, she spotted Talia.

Not wanting to be rude, she said, "Congratulations again,

Talia, on your company. Everything looked fabulous. I know you will do well."

"Thanks, Piper, but why are you leaving so soon? You're going to miss the prize giveaways."

"It's fine. I have some things to take care of at home."

Then she hugged Talia and was gone.

The following Saturday, Piper felt tense but happy. It was officially her last night working at Golden Bar. Originally she planned to work Saturday and Sunday but decided she would use the next day to treat herself to some spa services and dinner with Lish.

"It's your last night dancing, Piper! How do you feel?"

"Good and shaky. Like I'm taking off the training wheels of a bike for the first time."

"Why do you say that?"

"I just never thought I would have a career beyond stripping. Even when I got the job at the vet, stripping was still with me. Leaving this job makes it seem more real and final somehow."

"I get that, but you will be fine. You're already doing so great."

Piper looked down at her hands.

"Lish, I don't even know if I can support myself on that salary alone."

"You've told me that before, but you saved some money, right?"

"Yeah, I did."

"And you only plan to stay there for another few months before looking for a more lucrative position, right?"

Piper exhaled, smiling nervously.

"Yup, that's the plan."

"Well, then your bases are covered. Doing something new is always scary, but this is good, and you worked so hard for it. Not to mention, I'll help you if you get into any binds."

Piper opened her mouth but Lish cut her off.

"I know, I know you don't like people giving you hand-outs, but still, I'm here."

"Thanks, Lish."

Piper picked up the eyeliner and continued her tight line technique. It added a nice effect to the sultry eye look she'd perfected. Next was the contouring of her already high cheekbones. She used a slightly lighter shade than her amber-colored skin tone to highlight and followed up with one a tad darker to the hollow of her cheeks to create the chiseled look.

"I'm going to miss you," Lish said, adjusting one of Piper's loose curls.

"Lish, you see me all the time. Have you forgotten you are my best friend?"

"I know, but I won't see you at work anymore. It's so bittersweet. Who will give me my pep talks?"

Piper laughed.

"I got you covered, girl. Gus is going to step in."

Lish tried to punch Piper in the arm, but she dodged the playful blow at the last second.

Sobering her tone, Piper said, "I'll text you the pep talks, okay?"

"Whatever, I don't need you anyway. I'll find a new stripper best friend."

"Oh, Great! I think Lily is available."

"You mean Bunny Tail? Hell no!"

Lish smiled and put her arms around Piper.

"It's time for me to jump on stage, my dear friend. But I'm so very proud of you."

Lish touched her shoulder, and Piper patted Lish's hand. Before exiting, Piper called out to her.

"Lish," she said with a mischievous grin. "Get 'em hard."

Lish gave her a thumbs up. The line was one that she and Lish created shortly after they began working together. It was their good luck version of 'break a leg' that was so popular with actors. They figured the more turned on you got the audience, the more money they were likely to spend.

Piper finished up her makeup. As she was clearing off the setup station, there was a knock at the door.

"Come in."

The door opened, and Piper expected to see another dancer, the club's owner or maybe even Gus, having wandered his way downstairs. But to her total amazement, Scott walked in.

"Scott! What are you doing here? How did you get back here? Never mind," she said, rushing into his arms. "I'm just happy to see you."

He moved the bouquet of flowers he was holding before she crushed them.

"Hey, lovely. I know you told me this was your last night working here, and I wanted to be supportive, so I flew down for the night."

"When do you have to return?"

"Tomorrow morning."

It was only a short trip, but a short trip for her. She felt so special.

"This is so sweet and . . ." she shook her head. "I don't know what to say; this is such a great surprise."

Piper hugged him again, took the flowers from his hand, and placed them on her makeup station.

"How did you get in?"

"I parked in the back and was hoping to see you, but

instead, I saw another dancer come out. I asked if she knew you, and she let me in and told me where to find you."

The Golden Bar probably should do a better job with security, but Piper was too overcome with Scott's thoughtful gesture to care. He was wearing jeans and a red and black shirt. His full lips displayed an appreciative smile as he slowly looked her over.

"Do you share this room with anyone?"

"One other girl, but she's off tonight."

"Is that so?" he said, stepping closer to her and wrapping his arms around her waist.

"It is."

"You look fucking incredible. All the guys are going to be wishing they had you tonight."

"Maybe they will, but I only want one of them."

He laid a few teasing kisses across her exposed shoulder. Then slid the strap down to continue a few inches lower. Piper felt tingling in between her thighs and stepped closer to him.

"Care to tell me who he is?"

"I can give you a hint," she said, pulling him closer and kissing him with all the intense heat she had been holding in since the last time she saw him.

Breaking the kiss, but his lips still only inches from hers, he asked, "How long before you go on?"

"Ten minutes."

"I can make that work."

He lifted her onto the table and yanked off her underwear. His movements were fueled by a desire to own her body completely. Matching his eagerness and desire, Piper undid his jeans and instantly freed his throbbing dick. She grabbed hold of it and began massaging it with her hand.

Scott pushed her against the mirror and thrust into her. Already wet and turned on, the pleasure she felt made her react without thinking, planning, or restraint. She wanted him so bad and sunk her fingers firmly into his ass to pull him deeper.

His dick was massively hard and slick from her pussy. The idea of him fucking her in a room where anyone could walk in and enjoy the show made their risqué behavior even hotter. His movements were firm and unforgiving, and she liked it, begged for more of it. Her climax was rapidly approaching, and her back tightened as Scott continued taking what she now considered his.

"I'm about to come. Don't stop," Piper begged.

But suddenly, he did.

Her eyes popped open as her chest rose and fell.

"What . . . are you . . . doing?" she asked in between breaths.

He withdrew from her and buckled his pants.

"We can finish when your show is over. Right now, I want you on that stage with your pussy wet, your nipples hard, and your mind locked on me."

She nodded and yanked him to her for a long, sweet kiss. While doing so, he placed one finger into her pussy, moving it slowly and deliberately teasing her again and covering it with her juices. Ending the kiss, he placed his finger into her mouth, and Piper moaned and sucked, enjoying the taste of herself on him.

"Time to go sexy," he said, stepping back.

Piper pulled her underwear back on, slipped down from the table, and winked at Scott before leaving the room.

CHAPTER 5

"**L**ook at that chest," Lish said, watching the tall, muscular, shirtless man lift boxes outside. He was the new guy moving into apartment 2D.

"I'd like to lick things off of it."

"Hmm, I can see why," Piper responded.

Lish swatted her hand.

"No, you stop it. You have Scott. This one is for me."

"Fine by me," Piper said, getting off the couch. "You can have him. I'm sure he isn't as sweet as my Scott anyway."

Lish continued to stare, unaware that Piper had even moved.

"They put him in the right apartment."

"Why do you say that?" Piper asked.

"Because D stands for dick, and I'll bet he has a big one! I'd suck him dry."

Piper laughed.

"That I can believe. You want a drink?"

Lish licked her lips and put one hand on the windowpane.

"I sure do."

"A real drink nasty. Not whatever your mind is conjuring up."

"I said yes! What are you making?"

"In honor of your use of the letter D, how about I make some Daiquiris?"

"Perfect."

Piper pulled out the blender and ingredients for two strawberry Daiquiris.

"Tomorrow, do you—" Piper stopped mid-sentence. She looked up to see Lish still staring out of the window and practically drooling.

"I have some condoms in my room if you need them."

Peeling her eyes away from the window, Lish moved down further onto the couch, picked up her purse, and pulled out her cellphone.

"What are you doing?"

"That man has me all hot and bothered, so now I have to send Troy a text about coming over later tonight."

"Of course, you do. Are you free tomorrow?"

"Nope. I have to pay some bills, run errands, and drop off groceries at my mom's house, all before work. Why?"

"I was thinking about going lingerie shopping and wanted your company."

"Lingerie shopping? I thought you were watching your spending?"

"I am. I only wanted one cute, sexy piece."

"You considering giving Scott the goods?"

When Piper didn't say anything, Lish immediately pounced on her.

"You've already slept with him, huh?"

"Twice."

"Twice?!"

"Yeah, my last night at the club and then again after we left."

"And you didn't even tell me? How was it? He doesn't have one of those disappearing act dicks does he?"

The disappearing act dick was the description Lish gave to men with small members.

Answering her friend's questions in order, Piper said, "I would have, eventually. Fantastic and NOT AT ALL."

"Look at you. Kissing and not telling. You're growing up on me, Piper Fosters."

Piper smiled but then froze when Lish said her next words.

"Just be careful."

"Why do you say that?"

"No reason."

"Don't say no reason. It is clearly something."

Lish sat up straighter on the couch.

"I don't want you to move too fast."

"Me, move too fast? Coming from you, the one who has screwed on the first date multiple times?"

"Yeah, I have, but I'm not talking about the sex. I'm saying I can tell you like him, which is great, but things are moving fast, and sometimes that can be a red flag."

"How are we moving too fast? I've known him almost a month now, we talk constantly, and since he's only in town a limited amount of time when we see each other, we have to make it count. Why can't it be that we have a connection?"

"It can be, but . . ."

"But what?"

"You've already met his son, spent the entire weekend together, and there's still a lot you don't know. Something might be off."

Piper couldn't believe what her friend was saying. Scott had been nothing but kind to her so far, and he made her happy.

"What exactly is off?"

"I don't know."

"You're doing it again. Come on, say it."

"Ok. Fine. He seems too nice. Like he's hiding something."

"You don't like him cause he's nice?" Piper asked. "You're making no sense."

"I didn't say I don't like him. I said that something might," she slowed to emphasize the word, then repeated, "do you hear me? Might be off."

"I hear you. It basically means you don't like him."

"Call it what you will. I'm your friend. No, I'm your best friend, and I'm merely telling you to be careful."

"Your lack of support is noted."

"Don't do that, Piper. You are making something out of nothing. I could be wrong. Maybe he is a great guy, and I'm paranoid. I have been in two abusive relationships, remember?"

"Yes. Paranoid, that sounds like you."

"As long as you are careful, I will gladly be that. All I want is for you to be happy and me to dance at your wedding."

"With clothes, right?"

"Uh, sure," Lish joked.

"Well, he does make me happy."

"Good! Now bring me my drink so that I can watch some TV drama."

Lish made good points, but Scott was unlike any man Piper had ever met. Although she understood the need for caution, it hurt that her friend wasn't entirely on board about Scott. Loading the ingredients into the blender, Piper did what she did best and pretended like Lish's words didn't bother her.

◆◆◆

"I bought you something," Scott said, holding out a box to her.

They had officially been together three months, and he was in town for his one-week visit.

"Oh wow. What is it?" she said, looking up at him.

"Why would I tell you that when you can just open it?"

Piper sat up in bed and opened the box. It was a gold tennis bracelet.

"This is so beautiful," she said, removing it from the box. "You did not need to do this."

"I did it because I wanted to. Nothing but the best for my amazing woman."

Scott helped her put the bracelet on. Then kissed her on the cheek. She loved him, not only for being so kind but also because he was the first guy who made her feel like she truly mattered.

They heard Ryan make a slight sound, and Scott stiffened, glancing over at the baby monitor. When Ryan remained quiet and seemed to fall back asleep, Scott relaxed.

This was the first time they had spent the night at his house, and Piper felt giddy and special. He had a lovely home. Small and cozy, with minimal decor, but nice. Simone, the live-in nanny, was gone until the next day, so it was only the three of them.

Piper hadn't met Simone, but already, she respected the woman a great deal. The house was clean and organized, and Ryan was such a happy, thriving baby. It was easy to see that Scott made a good choice in hiring her.

Glancing at the pictures on the wall, Piper's eyes locked on the one that stood out the most. It was a picture of Ryan with his mom. In the photo, Scott's deceased wife, Julia, held a tiny Ryan that couldn't have been more than a few days old. They looked so much alike from the eyes to the nose and even the same beautiful brown complexion. Piper's heart went out to the woman who never got the chance to see her baby grow older.

"Ryan's so precious."

"Yes, that's my little guy. I can't believe how big he's getting."

"I know. I've only known him three months, and even I can see how fast he's growing."

"Oh, and his walking is improving. Let me show you a video."

Scott grabbed his phone from the nightstand and played the video. Immediately Ryan's adorable smile sprang to life, accompanied by drool and babbling.

Piper couldn't see who was holding the camera, but she guessed it must have been Simone. Scott said she was in nursing school, and the person sitting on the floor with their legs outstretched was wearing scrubs and nurse clogs. Ryan was only a short distance away, pointing at a toy.

"You can do it, Ryan. You can do it," Simone cheered.

In another few seconds, Ryan made it to what must have been his desired destination because he picked up the toy and sat down.

The woman clapped, and the video stopped.

Piper touched her chest and melted.

"That was so sweet. I could watch it over and over again."

"I know what you mean."

Scott smiled, but somehow his eyes didn't quite hold the joy.

"You okay?" Piper asked, touching his hand.

"I'm fine. It's hard being away from him so often. I miss him like crazy."

"Don't beat yourself up about it. Ryan knows that you love him. I can see it every time he looks at you."

He gazed into her eyes.

"You are incredible. You know that?"

In response, Piper squeezed his hand tighter.

"Do you plan to ever stop traveling so much for work?"

"I hope to one day. Not sure when. The company hasn't had any openings in Georgia lately. When I first got hired, I had a position where I rarely traveled, but after Julia got pregnant with Ryan . . ." he paused and cleared his throat.

Piper could see the difficulty he had when speaking about Julia. It wasn't surprising because he did tell her that he didn't like to discuss it. She started to say never mind, sparing him from a trip down a melancholy memory lane, but he started again.

"I took this position because it paid more. We needed the extra money, and it was only supposed to be temporary, but . . . you get the rest. I hope my work doesn't affect our relationship."

"Scott. You're a wonderful man and father. I love how well you take care of your son, and we can get through this. Distance is no big deal. Do what you have to, and I'll be in your corner."

He laced his fingers with hers and then checked the time.

"I need to get you back to your place soon. I have some things to take care of."

"I know. I have things to get back to as well."

She really didn't but hated sounding too needy and like he was the only exciting thing happening in her life, although he was. When he picked her up last night, he'd already told her that it would be a quick overnight stay. It was a Saturday, the day before he had to return to Milwaukee. It made sense that he had a lot to do.

Piper, on the other hand, had no plans. Already she had been spending more than she should have, eating out, doing some light shopping, and occasionally picking up the tab for stuff she and Scott did.

Reigning in the spending for a weekend would be a smart

idea. Her savings was still pretty substantial, but it wouldn't remain that way if she wasn't careful.

"I love you, Piper. I have no idea how I got so blessed."

"I love you too," was all she could say before he covered her mouth with his. He placed his hands underneath her shirt and pulled it over her head. This would be the third time they'd made love in less than 24 hours, and it was still as hot as the first time.

Hands grouping, tongues licking, and sounds of ecstasy filled the silence that was in the room only moments before. Scott's eagerness to have her was always exciting. They both pulled and clawed at each other with a ravenous appetite.

His forceful yet deliberate thrusts were causing pulsating pleasures to spark all over. It never took Piper long to climax, and this time would be no exception.

A few minutes later, sweating, moaning, and clenching the sheets, her body released a series of delicious explosions that made one thing crystal clear. Scott Bolden was the only man she wanted, needed, or cared about.

Scott dropped her off at home two hours later, promising to call when he could. Entering the building, Piper caught sight of the new guy from apartment 2D, running with his dog. He was most undoubtedly attractive with a nicely toned body. He looked in her direction, and Piper averted her eyes.

Staring too long didn't seem right, but instantly thoughts of Scott filled her mind, and she forgot all about the new resident.

Before going upstairs, she went to her mailbox. Leo, the grumpy guy from 2C, was carrying three boxes of various sizes towards the elevator. He was an older guy, likely in his seventies, and it looked like he was having trouble. One of the boxes fell, and Piper picked it up.

"Hi, Mr. Leo, would you like some help getting those upstairs?"

"Why would I need help? You just want to steal from me. Don't think I don't know how you young kids are. Always stealing, lying, and having sex like rabbits!"

These were familiar rants courtesy of the irritable older man. He steadied himself on his wooden cane and eyed her suspiciously.

"Nothing gets by you. But I promise I won't steal anything. I'll merely take the boxes to your door and leave you alone."

"You can leave me alone now," he said and snatched the box away.

Then Piper wondered, could a person that moved a notch above a snail's pace technically snatch anything? It was more like he pulled at the box with aggressive intent.

Piper released the box and decided instead to help him with the elevator. After pressing the button, the doors immediately opened, and she held a hand up, preventing them from closing while he stepped in.

"I guess you want me to thank you for getting the elevator?"

"No, sir, just being the mischievous juvenile I am and helping out against your wishes."

"Good! Because I'm not thanking you."

Piper smiled to herself. Inside the elevator, he dropped another box, and she picked it up. Once again, he took it with implied aggression. After the doors closed, Piper hurried upstairs to meet her disgruntled neighbor as he exited.

"Oh, it's you again," Mr. Leo said in a tone filled with repulsion.

Stepping off the elevators, Mr. Leo made the slow but thankfully short walk to his door. Piper waited around in case he dropped the boxes again. Fortunately, he didn't, and as she expected, he entered his apartment without a word or even another glance in her direction.

Shaking her head, Piper opened her door, tossed the mail on the kitchen counter, and went to shower. Drying off, she heard the buzz of her cell.

"Hello?"

"Piper! Thank God you answered. Jake has been in an accident. Can you please come to the hospital?"

Piper felt like her heart had stopped. It was Daya, and she sounded terrified.

Something had happened to Jake? No, it couldn't be. Not sweet, innocent little Jake.

"Is he . . ." Piper was too afraid to finish the question.

"No, No, he's not dead. I'm so sorry I should have led with that. I can't focus. I'm down here by myself, and you are the only person I could think to call. Can you come and sit with me? I can't stop crying. I feel so guilty."

Piper got dressed, picked up her shoes, purse, and keys, and rushed out the door.

"I'm already out the door, Daya. What hospital?"

Daya provided all the necessary information, and they ended the call. The hospital wasn't far, and Piper arrived in record time.

The waiting room was full of people expressing all levels of emotion. Some were smiling, others were crying or upset, and a few sat quietly with distant looks in their eyes.

Piper approached the desk giving the staff member Daya's information. It took a few minutes to locate the room because it appeared Daya had written 'Day' on the forms as her first name , solidifying how mentally distraught she was.

Piper knocked on the door and heard Daya's voice tell her

to come in. Even before setting eyes on her, the stress and worry in Daya's tone were evident. Seeing her face only confirmed what Piper suspected. The woman looked defeated and exhausted. Piper had only seen her last week, now sitting here with Jake; it was as if she had aged five years.

Daya jumped up and wrapped her arms around Piper.

"Thank you so much for coming."

"Of course, I wouldn't be anywhere else. How is he?"

Daya turned to look at her son, lying in bed with monitors beeping and tubes everywhere. Piper felt sick and had to look away to prevent herself from breaking down. Watching her fall apart was the last thing Daya needed, so instead, Piper took a deep breath and pulled on her bravest face.

"He's better, not in a lot of pain and getting rest. I feel so guilty."

"Daya, this isn't your fault."

"But I should have been watching him. He wanted to go outside and ride his bike. The parking lot had too many cars, so I let him ride on the sidewalk in front of the building by the main street and . . ."

Daya covered her mouth, and Piper put her arm around her.

"It's okay. You don't have to tell me anymore. Have you eaten? Can I get you anything?"

Daya shook her head as tears ran down her face.

"I'm not hungry, only tired but I can't sleep. This happened yesterday evening."

Piper spotted a box of tissue across the room and passed a tissue to Daya, and the woman dried her tears and then began wringing her hands together.

"I should have never let him play near the street. I told him to stay back. I kept warning him, but then I got a call. A stupid call!"

She covered her face with her hands.

"Mistakes happen, but he's going to be okay. They will fix him up as good as new."

Daya started speaking a mile a minute.

"I'm a horrible mother, Piper. I can't care for him. The doctors said it will take a few weeks until he is out of the hospital. I can't leave him here alone, but I can't miss work. I don't have any family to call on, or any money saved, I use everything trying to take care of us, this is all my fault."

Piper pulled Daya in for a hug. The woman was shaking, afraid, and blaming herself for all of this. It broke Piper's heart seeing both Daya and Jake in this situation. There was no way she could stand by and not help. Daya began crying again, and Piper squeezed her tighter, offering the only promise she could.

"Shh, I'm here now, and I'll help you get through this."

CHAPTER 6

Piper stared at the computer and hit the refresh button. Nope, no changes. There was still only enough in her checking account for rent and bills. What was left could either cover an evening out or gas for the next two weeks, but not both.

Piper clicked a few buttons and navigated to her savings account. It was low, pathetically low. It had only been four and a half months since she stopped stripping, and her savings was close to empty.

How did my money deplete so fast?

The question was rhetorical, and the answer was simple. Spending. Shopping, treating restaurants like her personal chef, and little spends here and there were all things that she probably—no, definitely—could have done without.

However, the biggest reason for the massive dip in savings was one that she didn't regret. To care for Jake, Daya had to miss six weeks of work. With no money saved and no other family or friends that could offer anything substantial, Piper had gladly given her $2,500. Initially, Daya refused, but eventually, she had to accept.

Piper knew how it felt to be a child without their mom, and she didn't want that for Jake, especially in his time of need. Although Daya blamed herself for all this, she was a good mom and deserved to be with her son. Of course, Daya promised to pay her back, but Piper wasn't holding her to it.

It was her decision to help; therefore, any consequences would be hers alone to face. A reduction in frivolous spending would have to be the answer. That's all there was to it—no more unnecessary purchases.

This would be harder than she thought because stripping paid more. Piper was used to doing what she wanted when she wanted. All of this budgeting was unfamiliar and more challenging than originally expected.

At least on the bright side, Jake was better. He ended up spending three weeks in the hospital and three weeks at home. Daya started work again this week and would need Piper to start watching him again.

Feeling guilt for requiring so much help lately, Daya offered to pay Piper for watching Jake, but Piper knew Daya barely had any money herself. It was the whole reason she needed Piper to watch him in the first place so that she could afford Pre-K the rest of the week.

Lish was always around to help if she needed it, but Piper didn't like the idea of handouts.

Her mind traveled to Scott. If things got too severe, maybe asking him for assistance wouldn't be so bad. However, that would be awkward. She loved him, and he said he loved her, but things were still new, and she didn't want to give him the wrong impression of who she was.

No, her best bet would be to stick to her plan. Cut down on the card swiping and get serious about looking for another job. After all, she had officially worked at the clinic for a year now. She'd paid her dues—time to leave Mrs. Friedman to it.

Piper logged out, closed the screen displaying her laugh-able bank details, and opened up a site where local jobs were posted. Scanning the choices, two positions stuck out to her immediately due to their pay and close proximity to where she lived.

"Piper?"

It was Mrs. Friedman coming towards her desk.

Piper quickly minimized the screen for jobs and gave the woman a warm smile.

"Yes, Mrs. Friedman?"

"Can you please waive the overnight stay fee for Mrs. Kelly's dog? The poor guy passed away last night. He was just too old to hang on any longer. It doesn't feel right to charge her for the stay."

"Yes, of course," Piper replied, hitting the appropriate keys to pull up Mrs. Kelly's account.

"I will do it right now."

A worried expression etched Mrs. Friedman's face.

"Do you know that is the third animal to pass away this month? Lately, so many of the animals are moving on to their homes in the sky."

The news saddened Piper. The loss of a loved one was hard for anyone. Her mind attempted to pull away from the current task and settle on the continuous decline of her aunt, but she reeled it back in.

"I'll also send a condolences card."

"Thank you, Piper, you're always thinking. I like that about you. Anyway, I'll let you get to it."

She turned to walk away and then stopped.

"By the way, could you help clean the cages again before you leave today?"

"Sure thing," Piper said, offering a tight smile.

It was ironic the animals were moving on to a better place to escape their pain. Piper needed to move on to a better company to get away from her pain in the ass, Mrs. Friedman.

Jake and Piper were sitting on the couch when there came a knock at the door. She wondered who it could be. Lish was at work, Scott wasn't due to show up for a few hours, and the neighbors hardly ever needed anything.

She placed the blue colored marker on the coffee table and gently laid Jake's arm down on the couch. Per his request, she was drawing a ninja kicking a bad guy onto his cast. Or at least she was trying to.

It was hard for a person that didn't know how to draw to capture the essence of a live-action scene the way Jake wanted. Her version looked more like stick figures having seizures.

"I'll be right back, buddy."

Jake said nothing. The TV had his full attention, and it made her smile. Thankful that he was still alive and already back to his usual, rambunctious self.

Glancing through the peephole, excitement filled her heart, and she opened the door with the intent to jump into Scott's arms but stopped. Was she seeing things? Just like Jake, Scott was wearing a cast.

Piper grabbed his familiar black work bag and ushered him inside, then closed the door.

"What happened?!" She asked, touching the casted arm delicately.

"It's nothing, sweetie, only a minor work injury. I'll be fine."

"It doesn't look like a minor injury to me. You look like Jake's unfortunate twin. Come sit down."

She pulled out a stool and practically pushed him down onto it.

"What happened?"

"I was helping some of my coworkers with wiring. Unfortunately, the ladder I was standing on had a loose bolt, and I fell to the floor. It hurt pretty bad when it happened, but the pain only comes in waves now."

"When did this happen?"

"Yesterday."

"Yesterday? And you're just telling me now?"

"I didn't want you to stress. I already knew you were worried about Jake."

"That's no excuse. I can worry about more than one person at a time. Is your company taking care of your medical expenses? Obviously, this was their fault."

"Yeah, they are. Trust me, Piper, everything is fine. Thanks for being so worried about me, though. It's sexy."

He gestured for her to come closer, and she did, giving him a heartfelt kiss. Getting lost in the moment, she leaned in a little too far, and he groaned.

"Shit!" she said, jumping back. "Did I hurt you?"

His response to reassure her yet again that it was no big deal was overshadowed when Jake suddenly turned around, likely due to Piper shouting a loud expletive, and came over. Being a one-track-minded four-year-old, he skipped the introductions and immediately took an interest in Scott's injury.

"Cool, I have a cast too. Is something broken? Did it snap and pop? Mine did."

"Jake! Manners."

"He's fine. He's fine."

"Yes, it did crack but not too bad, but it is fractured."

"What's Fra-sur."

"Fractured," Scott repeated, sounding it out slowly for Jake.

"It's the same thing as a broken bone. Sometimes people just call it that."

"That's weird. Anyway, your cast is cool, but mine is cooler. Look, Miss Piper was drawing me a fighting ninja on it."

Jake held up his arm to show Scott Piper's masterpiece. Piper cringed at how horrible the drawing looked with more light on it, and Scott smiled.

"It's very cool."

Piper mouthed him a silent 'I love you'. Then out of nowhere, Jake knocked on Scotts cast, and Scott winced from pain for the second time in the span of a few minutes.

"Jake!" Piper shrieked, pulling the boy back quickly.

"What? I just wanted to know if his cast was as tough as mine."

"And now that you see it is. Please go sit down, and I'll make you some food shortly."

Jake shrugged and rushed back to the TV.

"Sorry about that. You okay?"

"I've told you, I'm fine. Especially now that I see you."

Piper placed her arms around him, exercising more caution this time.

"I can agree with that. Not that you need a reason, but why are you here so early? You usually spend this time with Ryan and come to see me later in the day?"

"I wanted to surprise you and Ryan is with his grandparents. That way, you and I can spend some quality time together."

"Nice. Are you hungry? I'm going to make Jake a sandwich."

"I could go for a sandwich."

She headed around to the fridge.

"Do you want everything on it?"

"I'm taking anything you're giving," he said. "Pun intended."

She peeked around at Jake, still immersed in his show.

Whispering to Scott, she said, "That's good because tonight I'm in a pretty giving mood."

After making the sandwiches, they all ate at the kitchen table while Jake talked nonstop about Scott's injury versus his own, karate fighting, and dinosaurs.

Eventually, Piper suggested they go outside and get some fresh air to get a break from Jake's incessant chatter. Once there, they played a light game of kicking the ball around since neither Jake nor Scott had full use of both their arms.

The game was progressing well, with Jake scoring more points for being able to kick the ball into the chosen area perfectly a whole lot more often than Piper or Scott did.

"You should be a soccer player, Jake," Piper complimented as he kicked the ball perfectly down a concrete path between two small trees.

"I am incredible," Jake agreed.

He went to get the ball, but as soon as he bent down to pick it up, he yelled and jumped back.

"Eww."

Piper and Scott rushed over.

"What's wrong?"

"Look, there's a spider. I hate spiders."

The creepy black bug climbed off the ball and onto the pavement.

"Look, it's leaving. We can play now."

"We could or . . ." Scott reached into his pocket and retrieved a blue and yellow lighter. Next, he lowered himself within inches of the bug and set it on fire.

Both Jake and Piper shrieked.

"What the hell, Scott?!" Piper questioned as Jake stared in horror, unable to speak or move.

"What?" Scott asked, standing back up. "No one likes spiders."

"That's weird, Scott. I don't think you should do that again."

"Babe, calm down. Boys like different things than girls do, isn't that right, Jake?"

Finding his voice now that the tiny creature was free from its torturous demise, Jake said, "I guess it was kinda cool," then added in a quiet voice, "but I don't like fire."

"I'm sorry. I thought it would make you laugh. I won't do it again, okay?"

Jake accepted Scott's apology and picked up the ball to resume playing. Scott joined him, but Piper remained where she was. Her questions and thoughts were flooding her mind a mile a minute, but one, in particular, made it to the surface loud and clear.

What in the actual fuck just happened?

Later that night, after Jake left, she and Scott sat lounging on the couch listening to low playing Jazz. They'd finished dinner and were talking about how fast Jake was recovering.

"He's such a cute kid. I had a good day," Scott said.

"I did, too, but that bug thing was disturbing."

He sat up and faced her.

"Are you still on that? I was playing around, and no one got hurt."

"That's not the point. Why do it at all?"

"My apologies, Princess Piper, nothing so alarming will ever happen in your presence again," he said sarcastically.

"Excuse me?"

"I'm joking, Piper. It's a joke, okay? I told you I'm sorry, I've said I won't do it again; what more do you want from me?"

Considering the question, she realized she wasn't exactly sure. There wasn't anything more that could be done. True, she didn't like spiders, and that was still a horrible thing to do. However, Scott had apologized, and did she really want to dwell on this all night?

"You're right. Thanks for promising not to do it again."

Settling back near him on the couch, she noticed he kept clutching his arm.

"Does it hurt?"

"Only a little here and there. The worst thing is the pain meds. They make me so tired it's hard to do much."

"I can imagine so," she said. His movements appeared stiff, and Piper's heart ached for him. She contemplated her next words carefully. They had never spent longer than a night together.

"Would you like to stay with me for a few days?"

Scott didn't say anything, and that made her feel awkward. Then she understood his silence was probably because of Ryan.

"You can bring Ryan. Or I could come to your house after work to help out."

He regarded her offer.

"Are you sure I wouldn't be a burden to you?"

"Not at all. Just tell me what you need."

"Staying here with you would actually be preferable. Ryan's grandparents came to get him right before I left, and Simone requested the week off, so it's just me."

"How long will the healing take?"

"The doctor said six to eight weeks."

"Are you going to stay in town the whole time?"

He exhaled.

"Sadly, no. Since this injury is work-related, I need to stay close by to keep visiting their appointed doctors. Makes the insurance process easier, I assume."

"So, how long do I have you?"

"Five days, then I have to get back."

She smiled and kissed him on the forehead.

"It looks like I got myself a temporary roommate."

She lay on his chest, and they resumed talking about Jake, moved on to Ryan, then talked about how they'd like to have a family together one day. Piper was excited. A whole five days with the man she loved was going to be heavenly.

Piper's week with Scott wasn't as heavenly as she'd planned. Truthfully, some days, it was more like hell. He hadn't caused any significant issues in all fairness, but being around him every day revealed a few things that made her eternally grateful when the week was over, and he returned to Milwaukee.

For one thing, he didn't clean up any messes he made. That wasn't such a big deal because he was hurt, and the goal was for him to relax. He even told her upfront that he probably wouldn't be much help around the apartment due to the meds making him sleepy. Even still, she didn't think not being much help literally meant he wouldn't help at all.

He left dishes, cups, chip bags, gum wrappers, and anything else he used on the living room table. In addition, there were dirty clothes on the bathroom floor and toothpaste and puddles of water all over the bathroom counter.

Every day after arriving home, she needed to clean up, take out the trash and give him his food. The kicker was that she gave him food before leaving for work, prepped his lunch, and left it in the fridge, but he never grabbed it.

Instead, he waited until she returned from work to bring it over to him while he lounged on the couch in front of the TV. He kept insisting that the medicine made it hard for him to do anything else. However, Piper suspected many of his mannerisms were present long before he had to take pain medication.

Another issue was that she had to once again tap into her savings. She was used to only feeding herself and Jake once a week. Adding another adult into the mix was costly because when Scott did eat, he ate a lot. Once the frozen burgers, hotdogs, and various other microwave meals were gone, Piper started ordering out and paid for everything because he said that not working for a while meant he didn't have the extra money to spend.

All and all, it was an exhausting, expensive week. Once she kissed him goodbye and closed the door, she breathed a sigh of relief that the houseguest from hell, aka the man she loved, was heading back to ruin his own place.

CHAPTER 7

The following work week was productive . . . for Mrs. Friedman. For Piper, it was a headache. Along with her original hired duties, cleaning out the cages had become something she was permanently responsible for four days a week.

Another new task assigned to Piper was running errands that Mrs. Friedman claimed were for the company, but Piper didn't buy it. If nothing else, the old lady was getting her money's worth out of a desperate employee.

Fortunately, Piper had officially been employed at the clinic for a year and would likely get a good reference. Unfortunately, searching for a new job was an effort that had yielded no results. Money was still tight, and something needed to change soon.

That wage increase Mrs. Friedman had dangled in front of her at the nine-month mark was only a lousy quarter. For all the good it did, her boss should have skipped the formalities and sent the 'raise' directly to the IRS.

When it was time to clock out, Piper practically ran to

her car, rushing home to do absolutely nothing, and she was very much looking forward to it.

Upon entering the apartment building, she made her usual stop to check the mail. There were a few envelopes and a package stuffed inside.

"Hi, there?"

Piper whirled around to see the gorgeous new guy from apartment 2D. He was holding onto the leash of a happy golden retriever. She'd seen him a few more times since he moved in, but usually at a distance. Seeing him this close made it plain that the distance didn't do him justice.

His skin was clear, his teeth were straight, even his eyebrows were somehow perfect but masculine.

Who in the hell had sexy eyebrows?

"Hi," Piper responded.

"I'm Desmond, but everyone calls me Des. This is Dagger. We just moved into 2D."

"Nice to meet you, Des. I'm Piper. I live in 2A." Then leaning towards the dog, she said, "Hi Dagger, aren't you just the cutest?"

Dagger collapsed to the floor, offering his belly for affection.

"He's such a big baby. He belongs to my brother, but my brother went away to college, and my mom can't take care of him, so I was next in line."

"That's nice of you."

"I guess, but Dagger eats more than I do. I'm thinking of sending him on his way."

Piper laughed.

"But he's so cute," she said, petting the dog again. "And I work with dogs all day, so that's saying something."

"Makes sense," Desmond said, nodding at her blue and yellow scrubs. "Do you like it?"

"It pays the bills."

Or barely, she mentally added.

"I've seen you around. How long have you lived here?"

Did he mean he was checking me out?

"I've been here a few years."

Piper was trying to keep her answers short. Even looking at him felt like cheating.

"Do you like it?"

"It's nice and mostly quiet."

She tucked her mail and package underneath her arm.

"Well, it was nice meeting you, Des. I'll see you around. Bye, Dagger," she added, waving to the dog.

"Same here, Piper."

Turning in the direction of the stairs, she could feel that he was still watching her but didn't dare turn around to confirm. Her man was only a phone call away, and there was no need to open the doors of temptation.

Unlocking her apartment, Piper was greeted by a mess. Dishes were on the counter, clothes were thrown across the couch, the floors hadn't been swept, and it appeared her plant was dying in the corner.

"Shit, I forgot to water it," Piper grunted.

Last week, caring for Scott and going to work proved that she may have wanted a family someday, but wasn't up to the challenge now. Better get started on cleaning before she found a reason not to. The kitchen was what needed the most work.

Piper loaded the dishwasher with dishes from the counter, living room, and bedroom. As soon as the last cup was loaded, her cell rang.

"Hello?"

"Hi, Girlie." It was Lish sounding chipper as usual. "What are you doing?"

Piper looked around the apartment.

"Nothing much, mostly trying to see if there is still a floor underneath all of this mess."

"Want some company? I could kill some time before work."

"Sure."

Ending the call, Piper continued the cleaning spree. By the time Lish arrived, the kitchen was spotless, the plant had been watered, and a load of laundry was in the washer.

"I thought you said your place was a mess?"

"It was. I've gotten it halfway fixed now, though. Last week, when Scott stayed, had me all out of sorts."

"He stayed a whole week? What about his son?"

"Technically, it was five days, and Ryan was at his grand-parent's place. Scott got hurt at work, so I was helping him out."

"Hurt?"

"He injured his arm."

"Damn, that sucks!"

"It does. Either way, I had a mess on my hands, but now I'm starting to see the light," Piper beamed, glancing around at the room.

"Need me to help with something?"

"You can clean the living room if you want. The vacuum is in the closet."

"I'm on it."

Lish moved towards the closet to grab the vacuum and stopped. Picking up the package on the counter, she gave Piper a disapproving look.

"I thought you weren't doing any extra shopping?"

Piper put down the glass cleaner and rag and walked to the counter.

"Oh, I completely forgot about this. It's clothes from my cousin's fashion party I told you about. It should have arrived a long time ago, but it was free, so I'm not complaining."

Piper tore open the thick envelope and pulled out the skirt that she fell in love with at the party. It looked the same. Since she was wearing thin shorts and a tank top, she decided to pull it on over her clothes. After doing so, she walked around in it a little and swirled a few times for dramatic effect.

"That is so sexy. I want one! But in a different color, of course. Do they have a website?"

Inside of the packaging laid a small card with the website information.

"Yup, here it is," she said, passing the card to her eager best friend.

The twins were right. Giving out some of their merchandise increased visibility and offered a better opportunity to build word-of-mouth sales.

"I'm going to order one tonight. I hope they have one in green I need some fun beachwear."

"But you never go to the beach."

"Maybe I'll start," Lish said, holding her head high.

Piper took off the skirt and went back to cleaning the table. Lish got the vacuum and began her task. After Piper finished with the table, she threw her paper towels into the trash. It was stuffed and needed to be taken out.

"Be back in a sec!" she shouted to Lish over the noise of the vacuum.

There were no acknowledgments of being heard but dumping the trash wouldn't take long.

Once at the chute, Piper lifted the heavy bag and placed it inside. It gave some resistance, so she had to lean in with both hands and push hard to get it down the hole.

On the way back, she heard someone climbing the stairs, and they had to have been wearing heels because Piper knew that clank, clank sound anywhere.

Right after opening her door, she casually spared a glance

over her shoulder. It was a beautiful tall girl, holding a box of food, and she was knocking on Desmond's door.

Piper hurried inside.

"Lish, come here," she whispered.

"Why? What's wrong?"

"Nothing. Come be nosy with me."

Not needing a second invitation, Lish raced over.

Piper looked out the peephole first and confirmed that the girl was still standing in front of apartment 2D. Moving over, she motioned for Lish to take a peek.

"Who is that?" Lish asked. "Her legs are long as hell. I need legs like that."

"I don't know. I think it might be Des's girlfriend."

"Who's Des?"

"Oh Desmond, that's the guy from 2D. I met him downstairs."

Lish leaned a few inches away from the door and stared at Piper.

"Why don't you tell me any of the good stuff anymore?"

"I have Scott, remember? I wasn't thinking about Desmond."

That wasn't entirely true. For a few seconds, her mind had dabbled in a little sexual role play starring Desmond.

"Yeah, yeah," Lish replied, looking back through the tiny hole. "You have Scott. Desmond has Legs, and I have—"

"A vibrator and a collection of old horny men at the club?" Piper offered.

"Pretty much." Then she perked up. "He just opened the door, and Legs looks excited to see him."

"Legs?" Piper said, testing the name out. "I like it. It fits."

"And now they're gone. A cute little nice to see you hug, and the door closed. Ugh, I'm so jealous. I'll bet she's already riding that dick like a wave."

"Don't worry, Lish. We will find you someone."

"Piper, please, I don't want anyone. I like being free. I only want to ride on Desmond's play stick."

Then she started dancing and moving her hips to some scene playing out in her head that Piper didn't dare question.

"Come on, silly, let's finish cleaning and find something to watch on TV. The only thing I can afford these days."

"I can take us out if you want?" Lish said.

"You could, but you don't have to."

"I want to. Name the place, and we will go."

Piper's mouth twisted to one side. It was one thing for Lish to do something nice, and maybe in a week or two, Piper could return the favor, but at this rate, she had no idea when finances would be back to normal.

"Let's finish cleaning, and I'll think about it."

"Suit yourself, stubborn girl."

Lish went back to wrapping up the vacuum cord, and Piper started cleaning her bathroom.

"Hey," Lish called out. "How's Jake?"

"He's a lot better. Only wearing the one cast now. Daya watches him like a hawk when he's with her."

"I'll bet. That has to be scary. What about your aunt? How is she?"

Piper stopped clearing stuff off the bathroom counter and stared at her reflection in the mirror. The last time she spoke to her aunt was a couple of weeks ago, and nothing had changed. The sadness of the circumstance seemed to dig holes in Piper's heart and fill them with emptiness and guilt.

Therefore, she frequently dodged thinking too much about her aunt's condition, and in turn, her avoidance made her feel bad. Was it wrong that she tried not to think about her aunt a lot? Allowing a few calls a couple of times a month suffice?

"When I spoke to her last, she was still hanging in there."

"Piper?"

"Yeah."

"You're not a bad person."

Piper came out of the bathroom to see Lish standing next to the closet, having just put the vacuum away.

"Why do you say that?"

"I know you. You are feeling guilty for not constantly being in your aunt's face. Every time something heavy has happened in your life since I've known you, you do that to yourself. Get really quiet before answering because you are judging yourself."

Piper stared at the floor.

"Everyone handles hard times differently. It's okay to do it your way."

"I suppose that's true," Piper said quietly, then switched the subject. "I need a break from cleaning. Do you want to have a snack?"

"Sure."

Piper went to the kitchen and grabbed two giant bowls. One she filled tortilla chips and the other with salsa.

They sat down on the floor and dug in. After a few minutes, the fast-dwindling bowl of chips and salsa didn't stand a chance. It seems they were both hungrier than either had realized.

"Thought any more about dinner?" Lish asked, shoving in another scoop full.

"I'm sure I can find something here."

"Didn't you let me borrow some blue heels not too long ago?"

"Yeah," Piper said, recalling the loan.

"Well, I broke one of the heels. It looks like I owe you now. Let me take you out to dinner as repayment."

She said it all so casually, Piper couldn't help but giggle.

"Very slick. Fine, we can go."

"Great, where? I can go to work a little late."

"Hmm, maybe, the place on—"

Lish's phone rang, and she held up one finger.

"Hold that thought."

It only took thirty seconds to know that Lish wasn't coming back anytime soon. The call was a girl named Morgan contacting Lish about doing a private party. Lish rarely did private parties unless she trusted the source referring her. Since Lish worked with Morgan often, they would be on the phone for a while discussing all the details.

Remembering that she hadn't checked her own cell in a few hours, she went to grab it from the kitchen counter and was greeted by an unread text message. It was from Scott.

Instead of responding to it, she called him. The phone rang five times before going to voicemail. If anything, the fact that Scott barely answered his phone irritated her to no end. His excuse was that work kept him so busy it was hard to answer.

A part of her wondered if she was stupid for even accepting this reason as an excuse. Then again, what was a relationship without trust? They loved each other, and there was no cause to question him.

It was like her aunt had always said, "Whatever you do in the dark will always come to light."

Piper believed that truth with all her heart. Thinking of her aunt, Piper realized that there was an amazing woman that she should call, and as long as her aunt had breath in her body, she would always answer.

CHAPTER 8

Piper was so close, and it felt amazing. She was on the edge of a powerful orgasm, ready to devour all of her senses.

"I love you," Scott said to her.

"I love you too," Piper replied as euphoria poured in.

Then suddenly, something went wrong, so very wrong. Scott's hand was around her throat, and she couldn't breathe.

Her eyes popped open, and Piper stared up at him. His eyes were closed, but he somehow seemed distant and unrecognizable. She clutched at his hand, trying to speak, break his hold or at the very least get his attention. None of it worked, and to her dismay, his grip only tightened.

"Scott," she squeaked it in a voice so tiny and strangled it was more of a sound than an actual word.

Scott was choking her. Why was he choking her? She dug her nails into his hand and tried to kick. But he still didn't let go. Yet again, he squeezed tighter, and now terrified, Piper fought harder.

What is happening? Why is he doing this?

Her eyes blurred, and she grabbed at his face, slapping him hard.

Scott released his iron hold, and Piper gulped in the air. Coughing and touching her neck, she stared at him, horrified but also angry.

"What the . . ." she stopped to cough, "fuck is wrong with you?"

He looked at her bewildered, and then compassion filled his eyes.

"I'm sorry, I thought you'd like that."

"Why would I like that?" She asked, exasperated.

He rubbed his forehead, appearing apologetic and embarrassed.

"I thought that maybe you'd like to try something different, you know, more exciting?"

"Like dying?"

"I would never hurt you. Why would you say that?"

He came to sit beside her and tried to look at her neck, but she pushed him away.

"Piper, sweetie. I promise I was only trying something that I believed you might like. I guess I went too far. Our sex is always kind of kinky. I assumed this would be okay."

Piper wasn't entirely convinced. She swallowed a few times and watched him. The man sitting there was Scott, *her* Scott. The one she loved, who had made her feel special since the first day they met. But for a moment, he was someone else.

"Why didn't you tell me you wanted to experiment with choking?"

"I thought that trying it in the heat of the moment would be more thrilling. As dumb as it may sound, I heard it can intensify the orgasm."

Her defenses lowered slightly. She'd heard the same thing,

about choking but that didn't mean she had ever tried it or even wanted to.

Finally, Piper repositioned to get closer to Scott. It was possible that things simply got out of hand. Nonetheless, he needed to understand that surprises that would cause her permanently leave her body, was not her idea of a good time.

"Scott, I'm not upset that you wanted to try something new, but a heads up would have been nice."

He moved even closer and traced one finger slowly up her thigh.

"I am really sorry. Is there any way at all I can make it up to you?" he asked in a gentle voice.

She couldn't be mad at him, he was so sweet, and when he touched her like that, all she wanted was to wrap her arms around him.

"Maybe there is something you can do," she said flirtatiously, sliding his hand in between her legs.

Rediscovering the orgasm that she had lost would be a good start, but tonight simply wasn't their night—and the cries of an angry baby Ryan confirmed it.

They both sighed and quickly got dressed so that they could check on the little boy.

He was standing in his playpen with tears running down his small plump cheeks. Scott picked him up and immediately began lightly bouncing and shushing him.

The combo was precisely what he needed, and within seconds of laying his head on his father's shoulder, the cries turned into low whimpers and then into silence.

"Is he asleep?" Scott asked after a few minutes.

Piper looked at the baby. His head was turned to the side, staring into space as he relaxed on Scott's shoulder.

"No, he's up staring and biting on his hand."

"It's the teething. Could you grab the blue case inside my tech bag?"

Piper quickly but quietly went to the bag and opened it in search of the case. Locating the bulk square frame underneath some folders, she began taking items out to access the box.

Scott came over.

"It's fine. I can get it."

"It's okay. I found it, it's right—"

The stack of folders she'd lifted slipped out of her hand and spilled onto the floor.

"I said I'll do it," Scott repeated in a mildly harsh tone. "Here, take Ryan?"

Piper took the baby and stepped away. What was going on? This was now the second time that night he had done something out of character.

Scott set the blue case on the coffee table and collected the papers swiftly. Watching him, Piper noticed what looked to be vacation brochures and various folders. One of them had the words 'Julia's life insurance policy' written across the front.

Didn't he say Julia died over a year ago? Why was he carrying her life insurance policy around?

After everything was back inside his bag, Scott opened the blue case to get something for Ryan and then plopped down on the couch.

"I'm really fucking up tonight, aren't I?"

"What's going on with you?"

"I have a lot on my mind."

"Anything you care to share?"

Ryan reached for him, and Scott took him and gave him a teething toy shaped like a carrot.

"I had to take care of a few things concerning Julia's death, and it has me in a sour mood, I think."

"I saw the life insurance folder. You mean stuff like that?"

He blew out a breath and switched Ryan to the opposite arm.

"Yeah, the company had some issues concerning the paperwork, and I needed to resubmit a copy of it. I told you I barely like to talk about it, and all of this mess with the company makes me practically relive it."

Piper completely understood. His wife was a sore spot for him, just like her aunt was for her. Not wanting to talk about things that cut so deep was something they both shared.

"I wish I could do something to help."

"You help by being you, and I'm so grateful to have you."

He took her hand in his and kissed it.

"I have a surprise for you."

"Really? Why?"

"Because you're my woman, and I love you."

She smiled to herself, feeling remarkably special.

"How much is your car note?"

"$500 a month."

"Alright, pass me my phone."

She did so, and her cell dinged a few seconds later. Picking it up, her eyes widened as she read the notification.

"Scott, this is $1,000," Piper stated in disbelief.

"Yup. Now you can pay your car note for two months. I got a bonus at work, and I know you said you've been having a hard time. You really helped me out when I got hurt, and I couldn't think of a better way to spend the money."

"Wait! This is all of it?"

"No. Most of it. The rest goes to Ryan."

Piper was shocked. Quentin had never done anything this kind and selfless before. Actually, none of her boyfriends had.

"Are you sure?"

"I'm positive."

Scott kissed her on the forehead and relaxed back into the couch.

"You know what this means, right?"

"What?"

"You're going to get some fantastic sex when Ryan falls asleep."

"We already have fantastic sex."

"True, but an unexpected $1,000 makes my hips move in ways I can't control."

"Lucky me," he said, grinning.

She scooted closer and laid on his shoulder.

"Hey, I also noticed some brochures with pictures of the beach. Are you running off to a beautiful island and weren't planning on telling me?" she asked.

"Nothing gets by you," he said, pulling her closer.

The next day was Sunday, and Scott had already said his goodbye that morning. Piper sulked around the house a little as yet another visit with Scott was over, and she wouldn't see him again for three weeks.

The thought was an interesting revelation about their relationship. Every time she saw him, almost a month had gone by. It made the timing of how long they had been together vastly different from how often they had actually laid eyes on one another.

Could I keep doing this for years? Would I have to?"

There were always questions but never any answers. Sitting down at the kitchen table with her laptop and cup of water, she pulled up a popular website used to apply for jobs.

Her finances had only worsened over time, and sadly, not one company had called for an interview. The money Scott had given her was a significant help, but she still needed more.

She found another position posted in search of an Administrative Assistant at a hospital. Automatically she felt discouraged because the first hospital hadn't called her back. Applying for a job at another one seemed pointless, but she couldn't let hurt feelings cause her to skip out on possible opportunities.

Piper read over the job details. They required a year of administrative experience and a college degree, both of which she had. Continuing to scan the information, a glimmer of hope began. The pay was good, the location was good, and it was a well-known hospital called Juniper Creek Medical.

Wasting no time, Piper completed the application and uploaded her resume, saying a quick prayer before hitting send. A few more companies were hiring, but none that fit her as perfectly as this hospital. Regardless, she filled out the applications and hoped one of them would reach out to her.

Her phone began to play Lish's ringtone. It was the instrumental version of a song that Piper could never remember the name of, but Lish liked it because it sounded like something you would hear on the X-files.

"What are you doing?"

"Looking for a job."

"What fun?" Lish said sarcastically. "See anything you like?"

"One company, but you know how it is. Submit your application and never hear from them again."

"Can't say that I do. I've been stripping too long to remember normal jobs. Anyway, I just called to see if you had a fun night with lover-boy?"

Piper thought back to last night with Scott. It was interesting, to say the least.

"It was nice," she responded, stretching the truth.

Then she thought about the choking incident.

"Lish, can I ask you something?"

"Always."

"Have you ever been choked during sex?"

"Yes."

"Did you like it?"

Piper could practically see Lish grinning.

"Definitely."

"Why?" Piper asked, confused.

"What can I say? I love for a guy to be in control, and the random chocking adds to it."

"You weren't scared he would kill you?"

Lish laughed.

"That's a bit dramatic. The guy isn't supposed to make you feel threatened. Only choke you here and there to add to the fun."

"So not being able to breathe at all isn't part of it? Isn't that the point of choking someone?"

"It's hard to explain. Yes, it is a brief moment where you can't breathe as easily, but it shouldn't be to a point where it is painful, and your eyes bulge out of your head. Why do you ask? Were you thinking of trying it with Scott?"

"No," Piper said automatically. She wasn't sure why, but she felt embarrassed sharing what had happened.

"I saw it on a porn and wondered about it."

"Oh, well, you two should try it. It can be fun. Just be safe with it. I've heard of some guys blacking out during their climax and killing the girl."

"And that doesn't scare you?"

"Nope."

Piper shook her head.

"Yeah. I like my life most days. I think I'll steer clear."

There was a knock at the door.

"Lish, I have to call you later."

They said their goodbyes, and Piper opened the door to find Desmond. He looked as attractive as always, but his face carried a worried expression.

"Hi, Piper. I'm sorry to bother you. I remember you said you work with dogs, right?"

"I do. Is everything okay?"

"I'm not sure. Dagger has been acting strange all day. We went for a walk, and at first, I thought maybe he was only tired, but now he won't take water or food. Do you mind coming to check on him?"

"Sure," she said, picking up her shoes and door keys. "I'm not a veterinarian or anything, but maybe something will stand out to me."

"Thanks," he said, waiting for her to lock the door before heading back to his apartment.

Upon entering his place, the first thing Piper noticed was how clean it was. There were a few random blankets over the couch, a stack of magazines on the table, and running shoes near the counter, but overall, it wasn't what one would call messy.

The second thing that demanded attention was the smell of yummy food. Piper had no idea what he was cooking, but her stomach very much wanted an invite.

"Dagger is over this way."

He led her further into the apartment, near the glass balcony doors. In the corner were a dog bed and a bowl of food and water. Dagger lay there, unmoving staring straight ahead. He didn't even try to get up to greet her for his beloved belly rub. Desmond was right. Something was definitely wrong.

"How long did you say he's been like this?"

"Most of the day. This morning he was normal, but as the day progressed, he seemed to get more withdrawn. Do you think he needs a doctor? I was going to take him, but not sure if I should wait a little longer."

Piper bent down close to Dagger. The dog only followed her with his eyes. She rubbed his head, and he seemed to shiver a little.

"He needs to see a doctor. I can't be sure, but sometimes sudden lethargy in dogs can be signs of an aggressive UTI."

"Okay, Desmond responded, "Is your job open today?"

"No. It's Sunday we are closed on the weekends. We do have a 24-hour clinic we refer people to. I can give you the name, number and address."

He went into the kitchen to grab a paper and pen. Piper wrote down the information and handed it back to him.

Leaning down close to Dagger again, she said, "It's going to be alright, big guy."

"Thank you so much, Piper. You've been more help than you know."

"Of course, I hope Dagger is okay."

"Me too," he said, shoving his wallet into his pocket and turning off the stove."

"You want me to walk you out?"

"If you don't mind. I'm going to carry him to my truck."

"Can I help with anything?"

He passed her his keys and picked up Dagger.

"Can you lock the door?"

They exited the apartment, and he told her which key to use. Next, they made it to his truck, and she opened the door. He instructed her on how to let down the seats in the back. It was a quick, effortless task and opened up more room than she had ever seen in a truck.

Desmond placed Dagger inside and closed the door.

"Don't forget your keys," she said, passing them to him.

"I owe you, Piper. Thank you again."

"You don't owe me. Just take care of Dagger."

Getting into his truck, he said, "Name it, and I got you whatever it is."

Then he cranked up the truck, entered the address into his GPS, and pulled off.

She had to fight it, really fight it because quite vividly, a few sexually arousing ways Desmond Ash could repay her came to mind.

CHAPTER 9

Piper had submitted so many job applications and still nothing.

Why did companies always swear they were hiring but never call back?

Or they never called me. Was I seriously that professionally unappealing on paper? Or am I not selling my skill set well enough?

Her resume had been re-polished eight times. For good measure, she consulted with her cousin, Chloe, who had a management position in marketing.

There was always the possibility that her future would remain with the clinic until she got old and gray, then experienced an unfortunate ending just like some of the dogs had. With her luck, she would likely keel over while she was cleaning the cages.

This situation was very discouraging but giving up wasn't an option; she needed more money. A surprise increase in her water and power bill this month had only made things worse. Finances had gotten so bad that Piper sold some clothes, shoes, and old electronics for extra cash last week.

The money from those items would buy her more time, but it wasn't a plan she could continuously rely on.

Eventually, she would have to resort to letting the miscellaneous things like cable, wifi, and streaming sites go if she wanted to keep eating and living indoors.

You could always return to stripping part-time, she thought.

Piper sagged in her chair. She had told her aunt that once she made it through school and stopped stripping, it would be for good, but from the looks of it, her old life was tagging along and threatening to overpower the new one she was trying to create.

No, she wouldn't do that. One of these damn companies had to call her back. If they didn't, she would simply learn how to live on the bare minimum.

After pressing several keys to generate thank you letters for recent clients, Piper took a second to look around. The office was quiet today, which was good. The 'never a dull moment' theme that had been occurring the last few weeks was overtaxing.

Several hours later, work was done, and home was the destination. A frozen pizza and some intriguing medical dramas awaited her, and she didn't want to be late. The only thing that would have made things even better was if Scott was around, but their time apart still had two more weeks to go.

As if he could feel her thoughts, her cell chimed with a message from him.

Scott: Hi beautiful. How was your day?

She loved that he texted her most days after work was over. It showed how much he cared and thought about her.

Piper: Now that I hear from you, it's perfect.

Scott: Are you free tonight? I can call you later after work.

Piper: Yes, I am.

Scott: Great! I love you

Piper: I love you too.

That small exchange made her feel better and less alone. Worrying about what he did and didn't do when not around her didn't matter if he could make her feel this special even from afar.

After arriving home, Piper showered, pulled on a shirt and underwear, and popped her frozen pizza in the oven. Since there were 30 minutes to burn before it would be ready, Piper had a quick phone chat with Lish, then checked emails hoping that a job had responded.

When no emails worthy of opening stood out, she decided to pull on some shorts and take out the trash. Immediately after dropping the bag down the chute, she turned and came face-to-face, well, face-to-chest with Desmond.

He was shirtless and looked like he had just finished working out.

"Hi, Piper."

"Hi," she said more to his chest than to him.

It was hard, ripped, sweaty, and Piper wanted to touch it. In fact, her fingers twitched involuntarily at the mere idea. They were trying to make her touch him, but that would be bad. Plus, she had a man, an amazing man.

An out-of-state man, her mind offered.

Piper shook her head to clear the thought.

"You okay?"

She finally looked up at him, but it took an effort to unglue her eyes from his chest.

"I think I'm getting a headache," she lied.

"Do you need an aspirin? I can get you one."

"No. I'll be fine. How's Dagger? I haven't seen you two since last week."

That was another lie; she had seen him. He was walking Legs to her car at the time. Piper had ducked inside of the building to avoid introductions. The last thing that she wanted was a meet-and-greet session with his girlfriend.

"He is much better. It was a urinary tract infection, just like you said. I was going to come by and thank you properly when I had more time."

"Properly?"

"Yeah. Give you a bottle of wine or something. Unless you had decided on a different idea for me to repay you?"

Piper's eyes had shifted down again.

What is going on? Am I this horny?

He was talking, but it was his chest that was carrying on the conversation. It commanded her full attention. Scott's chest most certainly didn't look like that. Scott was slim and had a nice body, but Desmond was built like a TV superhero.

He lifted his bag of trash.

"I need to throw this away. I have to get back to give Dagger his medicine."

"Oh, I'm sorry," she said, stepping aside.

He dropped the bag into the metal hole and said, "Maybe I can cook you dinner one night?"

Is he flirting with me?

No, he wasn't. He had a girlfriend. It was only her body trying to flirt with his. But, surprisingly, Piper was a bit reluctant to turn down the invitation.

"Trust me, you don't need to repay me. Anyway, I need to be going. Have a good night, Desmond, and give Dagger a belly rub for me."

She started towards the door.

"I will, and Piper."

"Yes," she answered, turning around.

"I hope you feel better."

"Thanks."

Hurrying back inside offered her safety from the sexy man that had her thoughts going wild.

Thirty minutes later, she was in front of the TV, on the edge of her seat, consumed by the dramas of medical emergencies. It wasn't until the second episode that she finally picked up a slice of pizza and took a bite.

Even then, she was staring at the screen wide-eyed and nervous. A guy had come into the emergency room complaining of extreme rectal pain. When the doctor did an X-ray, they found the leg of a wooden stool lodged in his anus.

It turns out he had fallen onto a stool in his kitchen that was positioned upside down. However, when he got up, a piece of the chair stayed with him.

"How in the hell did he not know part of a chair was in his ass!" Piper yelled.

After they got the man prepped for operation, the show went to commercial break, and Piper put her pizza down and went to refill her drink.

The last of the Sprite sat in a two-liter bottle on the counter. What was left didn't fill her glass, so she added ice. Technically it was still the same amount of soda, but for some reason, when the cup looked fuller, she felt like she had more—positive thinking at its finest.

Her phone rang, and she rushed over to it, assuming it was Scott, but the caller ID revealed the words 'unknown number'.

Figuring it was a telemarketer, she ignored it and started back for the living room, when the phone rang again.

The caller ID still read unknown, but this time she decided to answer.

"Hello?"

Silence.

"Hello?" she repeated.

Nothing.

Piper blew out a breath.

"I'm hanging up now."

And right before she pressed the end call button, Piper heard them say something that sent chills up her spine.

"I'm coming for you, Bitch."

"Do you have any idea who it was?" Lish asked.

"Not a clue."

"Hmm. Was the voice male or female?"

"I'm not sure. I ended the call before I could hear anything more, and they never called back."

"Wow. That's creepy. Got any enemies?"

Piper thought about it.

"No," she said slowly. "The last person I got into it with was my cousin."

Lish hit the table, catching Piper off guard and causing her to jump.

"There you go! It's probably Tina, that bitch."

Piper shook her head.

"That's not Tina's style. She's a lot of things, but gutless isn't one of them. If she had something to say, she would say it."

"Ok, then not the bitch Tina. Anyone before her?"

Piper was still drawing a blank.

"I got nothing, Lish."

"What about Lily from the club. Maybe she thinks you are a threat to her and Quentin?"

"Why would she be calling now? I haven't seen Quentin or worked at the club for months."

Lish touched her chin and then looked up. A few seconds later, her eyes fixed on Piper.

"That's true. Do you think—" Lish stopped mid-sentence and tilted her head.

Piper knew exactly where Lish was going with this, and truth be told, she wondered the same thing.

"You are going to ask me about Scott, aren't you?"

"Yeah," Lish said fiddling with her fingers. "You think it was about him?"

"I don't know. It crossed my mind."

"Have you talked to him?"

"I spoke to him probably an hour after the call."

"Did you mention it to him?"

"No."

"Why not?"

"I didn't think there was a need to. Ultimately, I decided this probably has nothing to do with him."

"Is that really how you feel? Or is that your abandonment issues talking?"

"Abandonment issues?"

"Piper, come on. You know how you are. Your mom abandoned you, and although you've made an extraordinary life for yourself, you still have a leftover weakness."

"And what is that?"

"You hate to feel like you are turning your back on people the way your mom did you."

"I'm not like that," she said. Then more unsure of herself, she added, "am I?"

"Yes. That's why you stayed with Quentin so long. That's why you helped Daya and anyone else in your life that needs you. And that's why even if Scott is guilty you're going to see the good in him to avoid cutting him out."

Placing her hands on her hips, Piper eyed her best friend.

"What makes you an expert?"

"Because I have the same issues. You're 26, and I'm 28.

Two years may not seem like a lot, but it's given me more time to self-evaluate, and sad to say, I have issues."

"I could have told you that," Piper said with a laugh.

"Looking at others is easy. Can you see that about yourself is the question?"

"I can admit you may have a point, but that still doesn't make Scott guilty."

Lish watched Piper for a few seconds. Piper cared for Scott and would give him the benefit of the doubt, at least for now. Only time would tell if he truly was hiding something.

"Alright then. Maybe it was just someone pulling your leg or the wrong number."

"I hope so."

"Want to go do something fun?" Lish asked.

"Does it involve money?"

"Yes. But I will pay."

"No, I don't want you paying. There will be no more pleasure spending for me until I get extra cash."

"That's so boring."

Piper shrugged and picked up a fashion magazine she borrowed from work; if borrowing means you took it without asking over six months ago.

"It's my new life. Besides, it's not so bad. I do things at home to stay busy."

Lish looked doubtful.

"What do you do besides watch TV?"

"I do crossword puzzles, paint my toenails and play solitaire on my computer."

"Woman, are you 26 or 75?"

"Most day's I'm not sure," Piper joked. "Oh, wait! I did read something about a free concert on the lawn downtown. Want to go there?"

"Who's playing?"

"I have no idea."

"You know what? It doesn't matter—anything to get you out of this apartment. I don't want your old ways rubbing off on me," Lish said, standing up.

"Alright, Alright, I'll go get ready."

"Great! And I'll call us a ride because I'm getting you drunk tonight."

CHAPTER 10

Piper felt like it had been the longest three weeks of her life, waiting to see Scott again. They had officially been together a little over five months, and hardly seeing him was stressful and complicated.

Absence might make the heart grow fonder, but it made her mind go to some indecent places with the gorgeous man from 2D.

Piper jumped into Scott's arms and covered him with kisses as soon as he stepped inside the doorway.

"Someone missed me," he said, kissing her on the cheeks and then the lips.

"I did." Piper looked around. "No Ryan?"

"No. He's with the nanny. I'll stay with you a couple of days and then get back to him. I figured we need some alone time."

"You figured right," Piper hummed, putting her arms around him.

He dropped his bag right near the front door, and Piper tried not to let it bother her. He was just getting there. He was likely tired from work and not even thinking about it.

Going to go pick it up and take it near the bedroom, she asked, "What are we doing tonight?"

"You mean besides me bending you over that table?" he asked.

Her tone was flirty and playful when she said, "I'm ready for that when you are."

"Let me get some rest first, and then I'm all yours."

Piper stared at him in disbelief.

"You're about to go to sleep? You just got here."

"Doesn't stop me from being tired."

Scott picked up his book bag and walked into her bedroom. After removing his shoes, he lay down in bed. Piper was still shocked. Lish was right; obviously, she was 75.

"Scott!"

"What?" he asked in a slightly snappy voice.

Piper took a step back.

"Oh, I'm sorry, is it me that's annoying you? Here I thought it was the other way around."

Scott sat up in bed and patted the space beside him. Piper reluctantly walked over to take a seat.

"Baby, I'm sorry, okay? I've had a long few workweeks, and I haven't gotten much rest. If you let me take a nap for an hour, I promise we will do something when I get up."

"Like?" she said, prompting him to go on.

"Like I'll take you out to a nice dinner. After that, we can go for a walk and talk."

She felt herself softening.

"Can we go to a restaurant near your place and afterward spend the night there?"

Scott stiffened.

"No, I'd much rather stay over here with you. My area is like an hour away, and your place is more comfortable than mine."

"Are you serious? Your house is so cozy, and I've only stayed there once. I'm tired of always being at my place."

"I know, but it's quieter here. We will stay there another time, I promise."

She didn't want to push anymore. They were just now successfully circling away from the argument.

"Can we at least grab food over that way? I saw so many interesting restaurants the last time I was out there."

Piper fought the urge to emphasize the words "the last time" because it was technically the *only* time Scott had taken her to his house. In the past, she never pressed him about it because they didn't see each other often, and it shouldn't matter where they stayed as long as they were together, but the longer they were apart, the longer she had time to think.

"Piper, that's a far drive."

Batting her eyes at him and seductively tracing a finger over his chest, she knew the exact moment he had decided to give in.

"Fine," he sighed.

It took three hours to get to the restaurant. Instead of sleeping for an hour, Scott slept for an hour and a half. Once he was awake, it took 30 minutes for him to get showered and ready and another hour for them to get there.

Piper kept feeling like he was trying to stall but pushed it out of her mind. Scott had no reason to linger, plus too much negative thinking could ruin a perfect evening. An enjoyable outing with the man she loved was a way of revisiting her old friend, spontaneity. Nothing was going to wreck this.

By the end of the night, not creating any more issues was beyond worth it. Scott had taken her to NuVive, a classy restaurant with a candlelight dinner and a live jazz band.

They talked, sipped wine, and even shared dessert. This night was the exact type of outing that Piper needed.

"Are you ready to take that walk, beautiful?" Scott asked.

"Yes. I saw a lake shortly before we got here. You think we can go there?"

"That would be perfect."

He raised his hand for the waiter to bring the check. The server brought it over and bowed out gracefully as the jazz band was gearing up for another song.

"Oh shit," Scott said.

"What's wrong?"

"I forgot my wallet."

He stood to recheck his pants pockets as well as his jacket. Producing nothing, Scott rubbed his hand across his face.

"Damn it! I can't believe I did this. I was supposed to be taking you to a nice dinner, and I fuck up like this."

People were starting to stare.

"Scott, it's okay," Piper said, touching his hand. "I'll pay for it."

Lowering himself back into his seat, he said, "But you shouldn't have to."

He said more than a mouth full there because not only shouldn't she have to, but Piper also wasn't sure if she could. Her paycheck didn't leave her much extra.

Picking up the black book that concealed the check, Piper peeked inside.

FUCK!

It was $103, and her account only had $140 left to make it until the next pay period. That may have sounded like enough, but there was still groceries and gas to consider. But what choice did she have? Maybe he could repay her.

"It's fine. You can send the money back to me."

He looked down at the floor, and Piper felt her stomach drop down there too.

"I can't. I was going to use the last bit of available funds on my credit card. Money has been a little tight for me. A lot of expenses lately with Ryan. I'm sorry you had to find out this way."

Piper closed her eyes exhaled.

Goodbye frozen burgers, hello bread and water, she thought.

Then picking up the booklet, she inserted her card and put it on the table for the server to pick up. Her sweet night had soured so quickly.

Scott spent the next two nights pretending everything was normal, and maybe for him, they were, but for Piper, things felt different. She still loved him, but there was too much about him, she still didn't know.

He said he was also having money troubles. The predicament was understandable but isn't that something people shared? He hadn't told her about his issues, and she had been equally elusive. When pushed beyond the basics, what exactly did they know about one other?

Hoping to change that, she tried to develop new things to discuss, but the disinterest on his part was unmistakable. The irritation in his mood was likely agitated even more when Desmond stopped by unexpectedly.

"Hi, Des," Piper said, trying to make her voice sound as nonchalant as possible. She could feel Scott's eyes on her from the couch.

The apartment wasn't big, and from the doorway, Desmond spotted Scott. He gave a simple nod in Scott's direction and focused his attention back on Piper.

"Hi. I stopped by to give you this."

He passed her an envelope shaped like a card.

"What is this?"

"My way of saying thanks."

"Des. I told you there was no need to do this."

Lifting his hands in surrender, he said, "Hey, I believed you, but Dagger wasn't hearing it. He hounded me until I brought it over."

She laughed and heard Scott clear his throat.

"Tell Dagger thanks," she said, holding up the card.

Desmond gave her a brief salute before heading back to his apartment. Piper closed the door and awaited the questioning.

"Who was that?"

"Just a neighbor saying thank you. I helped him when his dog got sick."

Scott nodded.

"You couldn't introduce me?"

Oh shit! Did I forget to do that?

Piper was so nervous with the surprise visit and the uncomfortable aura pulsating throughout the room that the goal was to get rid of Desmond as quickly as possible.

"I'm sorry. I really didn't think about it."

"I'll bet you didn't."

He stood and went to the fridge.

"The fridge is empty. You don't have any sodas."

"No. I need to go to the store."

And you drank the last one, she mentally added.

"Want me to go with you?" Scott asked

"That's not necessary. I don't have any money to go after paying the check at the restaurant."

Scott shut the fridge door a little too hard.

"Don't try to make me feel bad about that. I already said I was sorry."

"I wasn't trying to make you feel bad, I—"

He put up a hand.

"Don't worry about it. I need to get going anyway. I have to spend time with Ryan before going back to work."

He collected his things while Piper remained stunned in place. With his bag tossed over his shoulder, he kissed her on the cheek, mumbling a dry I love you and left. Piper didn't respond. She had a few words for him, but they weren't I love you.

Piper went to bed early with no word from Scott and awoke the following day, mentally drained. Nightmares of arguments and misunderstandings kept playing out in her dreams.

Opening the fridge, Piper recognized how right Scott was. It was bare. Odd how that didn't seem to bother him when he was helping her eat everything up. Grabbing two slices of bread and an almost empty pack of turkey, Piper grabbed a plate and laid the items on the counter.

Desmond's thank you card was still right where she left it. Piper opened it and was shocked. The card was simple. It was all black with gold glitter colored letters that read thank you, but inside was a $50 American Express gift card.

Well, now hadn't she gotten lucky. Not only was a trip to the grocery store in her future, but Scott also wasn't there to help her eat it all up.

"What do you mean it's declined? I have enough money in my account."

The cashier, a young, black girl wearing a Georgia Tech shirt underneath a red apron, gave Piper a pitying smile.

"I can run it again?"

"Please do."

The clerk swiped the card again only to receive the same outcome.

"I'm sorry. It's not going through."

There was at least $30 left on her bank card after buying dinner the other night. The total came up to $62, which meant after using the $50 gift card, the remaining $12 balance should easily be covered.

Piper took the card. A man with a cart full of groceries got in line behind her. With no time to figure everything out while standing here, Piper selected items to be removed not to exceed the $50 limit and went to her car.

After placing the bags in her trunk, she got inside and pulled up her banking app. The problem was immediately visible.

NuVive had charged her twice, and now her account was overdrawn. Performing a quick Google search to locate their phone number, she called them but received no answer. Waiting another five minutes, she called again, and the restaurant's chipper voicemail greeted her.

She spent the remainder of the day trying to reach NuVive to no avail. It would have been easier to drive up there, but the place was an hour away and would waste too much gas.

However, when no one answered by noon the following day, Piper decided to leave work early and solve the issue in person. She couldn't afford to have them keep her money any longer.

She hopped in the car and was delighted that the drive to NuVive was progressing quietly and with minimal traffic. Piper listened to soft playing music and thought about how crappy her love and financial life were when she heard the well-known tunes of her phone ringing.

"Hello?"

"Hi. My name is Morgan with Juniper Creek Medical. May I speak with Piper Fosters?

Piper turned the radio off and sat up straighter.

"This is she."

"Great. I am calling because you applied for an Administrative position with us a while back. Are you still seeking employment?"

"Yes. Yes, I am."

"Wonderful. I apologize for the delay. We are so backed up with things here it has taken us a while to sort through resumes."

Piper was smiling from ear to ear.

"No problem. I completely understand."

"I would love to set you up for an interview if you're interested."

"I am."

"We will be conducting interviews for the next three weeks. Within the next 48 hours, I can email you the details, including a time and date for your meeting. You can confirm through email if the chosen slot works for you, alright?"

Piper was still in shock.

"That's perfect."

Morgan confirmed the email address she had for Piper and wished her a wonderful day. The lady had no idea that because of that phone call, Piper's day would be wonderful. Parking her car at NuVive, Piper had an extra bounce in her step. Receiving that call made her feel magnificent and that, finally, things would start looking up.

Approaching the desk inside, she explained the issue, and immediately a manager stepped in to assist.

"I apologize. You said we charged you twice?"

"Yes."

"Do you have the receipt?"

"No, actually, I don't."

"That's okay. When did you dine with us?"

"About four days ago?"

"The time of day?"

"Evening. I think around 7."

"Ahh, yes, we had new staff trainees that day. They must have entered the information incorrectly. All I will need is the card you used, and I can pull the receipt using the card number."

"Thank you so much," Piper said, passing the card over.

The day had gone from bad to brilliant so unexpectedly. Stepping away from the desk, Piper walked to the window and admired what a lovely day it was.

She noticed a couple running to their car, holding hands. They seemed happy. In the back of her mind, the questions wondering if she and Scott would ever get to that level of blissful joy again, resurfaced. Things had been getting more and more strained lately.

Sharing news about this latest job opportunity should pour some happiness back into things. Once she got her finances in order, maybe she could help him with stuff for Ryan.

Hmm, that was odd, she thought.

The guy looked familiar . . . too familiar. Her ears seemed to perk up, and the hairs on the back of her neck raised. As if it were all in slow motion, the woman leaned in and kissed the guy right before running around the car to jump into the passenger side. The guy looked around for a split second and then got into the driver's seat and pulled off.

"Miss Fosters, we have taken care of the issue for you."

Piper didn't respond.

"Miss Fosters?"

She could barely hear the manager speaking because her eyes were locked in a spot that just seconds before stood a woman she didn't know and a man that she was angry enough to kill.

THE END OF BOOK 1

Are you ready for More?

Love is Sour (Book 2)
&
Love is Salty (Book 3)

are available at Amazon.
If you enjoyed this book we would greatly appreciate a
review on Amazon.

ABOUT THE AUTHOR

Nicki Grace is a wife, mother, and author addicted to writing, spas, laughing, and sex jokes, but not exactly in that order.

Luckily for you, someone gave her internet access, and now you get to experience all the EXCITING, SHOCKING, and HOT ideas that reside in her head. She loves to have fun and lives for a good story. And we're guessing so do you!

Read more about her and check out more books at nickigracenovels.com

ALSO BY NICKI GRACE

Romance

The INEVITABLE ENCOUNTERS Series
Book 1: The Hero of my Love Scene
Book 2: The Love of my Past, Present
Book 3 : The Right to my Wrong

The LOVE IS Series
Book 1: Love is Sweet
Book 2: Love is Sour
Book 3: Love is Salty

Thrillers

The Splintered Doll
The Twisted Damsel

Self-Help

The TIPSY COUNSELOR Series
The Tipsy Dating Counselor (Summary)

The Tipsy Dating Counselor (UNRATED)

The Tipsy Marriage Counselor

The Pregnancy Counselor

Printed in Great Britain
by Amazon

83419592R00078